MY
DOUBLE
LIFE

MY DOUBLE LIFE

Janette Rallison

G. P. Putnam's Sons
An Imprint of Penguin Group (USA) Inc.

G. P. PUTNAM'S SONS

A DIVISION OF PENGUIN YOUNG READERS GROUP.

Published by The Penguin Group. Penguin Group (USA) Inc., 375 Hudson Street, New York, NY 10014, U.S.A. Penguin Group (Canada), 90 Eglinton Avenue East, Suite 700, Toronto, Ontario M4P 2Y3, Canada (a division of Pearson Penguin Canada Inc.). Penguin Books Ltd, 80 Strand, London WC2R 0RL, England. Penguin Ireland, 25 St. Stephen's Green, Dublin 2, Ireland (a division of Penguin Books Ltd.). Penguin Group (Australia), 250 Camberwell Road, Camberwell, Victoria 3124, Australia (a division of Pearson Australia Group Pty Ltd). Penguin Books India Pvt Ltd, 11 Community Centre, Panchsheel Park, New Delhi—110 017, India. Penguin Group (NZ), 67 Apollo Drive, Rosedale, North Shore 0632, New Zealand (a division of Pearson New Zealand Ltd). Penguin Books (South Africa) (Pty) Ltd, 24 Sturdee Avenue, Rosebank, Johannesburg 2196, South Africa. Penguin Books Ltd, Registered Offices: 80 Strand, London WC2R 0RL, England.

Printed in the United States of America.

Design by Richard Amari.

Text set in Celeste.

Library of Congress Cataloging-in-Publication Data in.
Rallison, Janette, 1966– My double life / Janette Rallison. p. cm. Summary: When eighteen-year-old Lexi of Morgantown, West Virginia, becomes the body double of a famous pop star, she discovers that the girl she is replacing is actually her half-sister, and that their father is a famous rock star. [1. Celebrities—Fiction. 2. Identity—Fiction. 3. Singers—Fiction. 4. Popular music—Fiction. 5. Sisters—Fiction. 6. Fathers and daughters—Fiction.] I. Title. PZ7.R13455Mxn 2010 [Fic]—dc22 2009034954

ISBN 978-0-399-25262-4

1 3 5 7 9 10 8 6 4 2

To my dad, who was always there for me. When I didn't think I was good enough to be a writer, he proved me wrong by sending an essay I'd written to a magazine. It was my first sale and my first step on this very fun road I now travel. Thanks, Dad!

And to my mom, who is the most avid reader I know. It's an honor to be your favorite author!

CHAPTER 1

I didn't want to write this. Really, there's a lot that's happened in the last few months that I'd rather forget. But Mom says I need to have an autobiography on hand, that I need to record all the facts, in case someone writes a trashy tell-all book about me. Mom also told me I should describe her as ten pounds thinner, looking like a fashion model, and being an immaculate housekeeper. So here's the disclaimer: Whatever else you might think about the events in this story, please keep in mind that my mom is gorgeous and our bathrooms were always clean.

Because autobiographies have pictures, I'm supposed to go through my photo album and come up with some representative snapshots that show what I was like before my life got swept away in stardust and celebrity glitter. None of the photos I have are truly representative of me though.

A snapshot couldn't reveal what it's like to grow up half white, half Latina in small-town West Virginia, or how missing your father your entire life changes everything. I could put in a picture of me sprawled on my couch with my best friend, Lori, but you wouldn't catch the crucial details: that everything I'm wearing and the couch itself are secondhand. My brown shoulder-length hair always looks the same, not because I have a no-nonsense style, but because it was the only style my mother knew how to cut. I was too poor to go to a salon.

Since I don't have a picture, I will describe a scene from my life, a day at the end of February when I asked Trevor Wilson to the Sadie Hawkins dance, the day that set so many other things in motion.

It started with Hector Domingas trailing me around the library. Since I'm bilingual, teachers always assigned me to sit by the Spanish-speaking kids who struggled with English. That way they had someone to explain anything they couldn't understand. In world history that person was Hector.

I helped Hector a lot. And because the Morgantown High staff might someday read this, I won't say more about his homework or any part I played in the completion of several five-paragraph essays.

The thing about Hector was that the last couple of days he'd been acting strange. He'd say bizarre things to me and then wouldn't explain himself. He'd show up outside my classes and watch me walk past him. It was beginning to creep me out, and I wanted to spend as little time with him as possible, but on this day Hector needed help on our latest writing assignment: *Leaders Who Changed the World.* He wanted to do one about Cesar Chavez. Unfortunately, Hector couldn't find any books on Chavez, and our teacher said we had to use books, not Internet sites.

I fingered the book I'd picked up on Churchill. "Choose

someone else," I told him. *"Solo escoge un libro del estante."* Just pick a book off the shelf.

"Deben tener Chavez." They should have Chavez. He folded his arms over a T-shirt that was too big. Hector never seemed to fill out his clothes. He was shorter than me— and, granted, I'm five foot eight, but with his skinny arms and large brown eyes, he looked like a freshman instead of a senior.

"You can ask the librarian to find a book for you," I said. I knew he wouldn't. He hated conjugating enough English verbs to pull off a conversation with a teacher. He scowled at me, then turned and disappeared down one of the non-fiction aisles.

I did a quick check around the library to see where Trevor was. He sat at one of the tables in the middle of the room taking notes. His blond hair stayed perfectly in place, even though he was bent over a book. It was like his hair just knew what to do to make him look good.

My plan had been to sit down at the same table and strike up a conversation. I walked several steps toward him, felt my stomach bang into my ribs, then made a U-turn and hurried over to the table where Lori sat.

She had several books spread out in front of her but shook her head with disappointment as I sat down. She'd watched me head toward Trevor's table and then bail out.

"Sadie Hawkins is nineteen days away," she said.

She had reminded me to ask Trevor to the Sadie Hawkins dance every day for the last week. She kept suggesting cute little ways I could do it, like bringing him Chinese food and engineering a fortune cookie with a slip of paper that said *I'd be fortunate if you went to the dance with me. Please say yes.*

Personally, I think asking a guy out is hard enough without turning the whole thing into some sort of reality show event. If you make it into a treasure hunt and he decides he doesn't like the treasure, well, how humiliating is that?

Lori hadn't asked anyone to the dance yet either. She wanted to double with me but couldn't decide between three guys who kept calling her. Picking one guy would mean choosing a favorite and thus offending the other two. Lori's life is so hard.

"I'll ask him," I said. "I just need to do it my way. You know, really casually."

She leaned toward me over her books and papers. "You're waiting for someone else to ask him so you don't have to. You're afraid to talk to him."

I glanced at Trevor, then quickly glanced away so he didn't catch me staring. "I am not."

She took a *Seventeen* magazine from her bag and slid it across to me. "Exhibit one: the flirting quiz."

I never should have taken that stupid test. Lori wasn't going to let me forget that I flunked it.

Apparently if you see someone attractive staring at you, you're supposed to either A) smile back at him playfully or B) send him a wink, not C) assume you have a wardrobe malfunction and check to make sure everything is zipped and buttoned.

And if a guy comes up to you and stands too close—it might mean A) he's interested in you, instead of C) he's trying to intimidate you by violating your personal space and you have every right to shove him away.

Luckily, *Seventeen* also wrote a "Rev Up Your Flirting Skills" article to remedy my near-hopeless situation. Lori made me read it. Three times.

Lori took a stealth glance at Trevor. "He's alone. This is the perfect time to ask him."

"I don't even know if Trevor likes me."

Which was my major problem. Trevor seemed interested in me during physics when he turned around at his desk to talk to me. Half the time he offered up some pointless trivia or made observations on my handwriting. He'd grab the pencil out of my hand and doodle comics on my assignment. Guys don't do that sort of thing unless they want your attention.

But at lunchtime, I morphed into the invisible woman. He didn't look at my table. He never spoke to me. Instead, he spent most of his time trying to get attention from Theresa Davidson, reigning popularity queen. He and his friends sat at the table next to hers and he'd do things like flip Cheetos onto her table. Theresa and her friends pretended to be annoyed about this, but they weren't.

If it were anyone else that Trevor was flirting with, I

would have accepted the fact that I had a rival and I would have tried harder. But Theresa and I had a history of bad blood. Back when I was a kid, we lived in an apartment in a rundown section of DC, and I was kind of a fighter. Not a gang member or anything; it's just that you had to be tough to get left alone. Now that I think about it, I guess I did get in a couple of fights in the beginning of sixth grade, because that's what convinced Mom that we needed to move back to Morgantown, West Virginia. She wanted a better environment for me. We've lived with my grandmother, my *abuela*, ever since.

Before I moved, my friend Armando told me, "I've been the new kid lots of times. What you need to do is figure out who the biggest bully is and take him on right away. You take on the bully, and it don't even matter whether you win or not because everybody knows you got guts and you don't back down. They'll respect you, and you'll fit in."

When I made my entrance into my new school, I instantly pegged Theresa as the biggest bully. After all, the entire sixth grade seemed to hover around her, waiting to do her bidding. So there was this unfortunate incident where she cut in front of me in the lunch line and I pushed her, causing her to stumble into a cafeteria garbage can.

Apparently that's not the best way to make friends at your new school. And this is the main reason I never take advice from guys anymore. They just live in different worlds.

Even though I apologized, Theresa and her friends never forgave me. They loved to remind everyone that I lived in a run-down neighborhood, that I walked to school instead of driving my own car, that I didn't wear designer clothes—there are so many ways to rub in being poor. I retaliated in the only way that wouldn't get me kicked out of school. I got straight A's so I could look down at them for being stupid. I probably owe all my high school honor roll achievements to Theresa and the Cliquistas. Oh, and that's another way I retaliated. I called them the Cliquistas. It's not my fault the name stuck.

Well, maybe it was my fault, but still, I refuse to feel guilty about it.

I looked over at Trevor's head, still bent over his books. So did he like me or Theresa? Maybe his throwing Cheetos at her wasn't really flirting. After all, I'd throw a lot of stuff at her if I thought I could get away with it. Besides, Trevor was in honors classes and Theresa's grades were much closer to mid-alphabet. How could he like someone who reveled in her own mediocrity? Then again, if he liked me, why did he always ignore me at lunch?

"He likes you," Lori said. "You're smart and gorgeous. For heaven's sake, you look like Kari Kingsley. How many people can say that?"

"Me and Kari Kingsley."

"Right. So turn on some of the celebrity charm and go talk to him."

I raised my eyebrow at her. I wasn't sure whether she meant to be ironic or not.

You know how they say everyone has a twin somewhere in the world, a person chance has formed to be their mirror image? Mine happens to be rock star Kari Kingsley. Our faces are eerily identical. In all the pictures of her that I'd studied, I'd only been able to see two differences: Her nose was sharper than mine, and she had blond hair. Mine is brown. But even that wasn't a true difference; her hair is bleached. Natural blondes don't have our olive-toned skin and dark brown eyes.

I'd think we were twins separated by birth, but Kari Kingsley is twenty-one and I'm eighteen, plus I'm pretty sure my mom would have remembered giving birth to twins and then losing one somewhere along the way.

When Kari's first album came out and her face popped up everywhere, I thought I was lucky to resemble her. She's beautiful, confident, and oozes sultriness. But then she opened her mouth and started speaking to reporters.

While walking down the red carpet on the way to the Grammys, a reporter asked her what she was doing to be green. She gave a dazzling smile and replied, "Nothing. I don't really celebrate Saint Patrick's Day."

During the MTV awards she put in a plug for the ethical treatment of animals: "It's so important we all remember that animals are people too."

Really? How many of us lick ourselves clean?

On *Good Morning America,* while talking about the reasons role models shouldn't smoke, she said, "Cigarettes can kill you, and that really changes your life."

I suppose so.

That's when it became a lot less fun to look like a celebrity. Her gaffes were instantly put on YouTube and half the senior class's Facebook pages.

Suddenly I was stupid by association.

I looked at Lori and tilted my chin down. "I'm supposed to turn on some of Kari's celebrity charm? I could tell him I wish I had some pickup lines, but my family doesn't own a truck."

She gave my arm a shove. "You know what I mean. Go bat your eyelashes at him."

I have never batted my eyelashes at anyone. Suddenly I wondered if that was part of the problem. Perhaps Trevor didn't realize I liked him. I couldn't blame him for flirting with Theresa if he didn't think I was interested.

I opened the magazine and looked at the flirting article again. I went over the bullet points in my mind. Maybe they would work. After all, highly trained professionals who understood the male psyche wrote these sorts of articles.

Trevor pushed his chair away from the table and went and stood by the Roman and Greek history section.

Flirting tip number one: *Don't stay in a group. A guy may feel like he can't approach you because of your friends.*

Before I could talk myself out of it, I stood up and followed him. He didn't take his eyes off the books in front of him, which made tip number two hard to do: *Gaze at him from head to toe, then flash him your brightest smile.* I decided to go on to tip three: *Smooth a wrinkle from his shirt or playfully tug on a piece of clothing.*

I reached over and smoothed out the material on Trevor's shoulder, which must have startled him. He jumped about two feet.

"Sheesh, Alexia. What are you doing?"

I froze. I couldn't very well tell him I was flirting with him. "Um . . . you had a bug on your shoulder, a big one. I brushed it off."

"Oh." He looked around on the floor to check if anything was crawling away and took a tentative step backward. "These books have been sitting here so long they probably have spider colonies living in the bindings."

Tip number four: *Compliment him.*

"Well, your shirt is really nice, so you can't blame the spiders for wanting a closer look."

He peered over his shoulder at the back of his shirt. "What? Are there more on me?"

Why was this not working? I went on to tip five: *Make and maintain eye contact.* I also flashed him my brightest smile since he hadn't seen it while I did tip number two. "No, of course not. There was only that one bug, and it's gone."

He met my gaze, but instead of smiling back, he narrowed his eyes. "Then why are you staring at me?"

"I'm not staring at you."

"You are too."

Okay, forget the tips. Tips apparently didn't work with the guys in my school. I held up one hand as though taking an oath. "I don't see any more bugs."

It occurred to me in a moment of brilliance that I didn't need that article. I already knew what sort of flirting Trevor noticed. All I had to do was copy Theresa's body language— and I'd seen her in action for years.

Theresa has thick blond hair, which she uses to swish lesser mortals into submission. I have seen her hypnotize guys by merely running her fingers through it. She also leans up against lockers in this seductive way with one elbow on the wall and her hand intertwined in her hair, which makes her look like she's posing for a fashion shoot. Then she half whispers things to whichever guy she's talking to so he has to lean in close to hear her.

I tossed my hair off my shoulder, which Trevor didn't see because he was examining the shelf in front of him, taking a book off slowly, and turning it in his hands to make sure nothing jumped out at him.

"So, Trevor . . ." I hadn't wanted to bring up the dance out of the blue, but I didn't know how to segue from bugs to dating and I couldn't prolong this conversation any longer. It was better just to do it and get it over with. "Have you been asked to the Sadie Hawkins?"

He looked over at me, really seeing me for the first time. His voice sounded hesitant. "No." Hesitant was bad, but then his voice returned to normal and he shrugged. "Well, not yet."

I put one hand on the bookshelf, leaning against it. I couldn't duplicate Theresa's one-elbow pose, but at least I could borrow some of her nonchalance. "Do you want to go with me?"

As it turns out, you shouldn't lean seductively against bookcases. Half a dozen books pushed through and went flying off the shelf into the next aisle. Somebody called out, "Hey, watch it!"

"Sorry," I called back.

I hoped I hadn't hurt whoever was on the other side of the bookcase—which would have been my luck: I'd go down in history as the first girl from Morgantown High who induced casualties while flirting.

I turned back to Trevor, but he seemed more interested in the hole I'd created on the shelf than in answering my question. I peered through it to see what he was looking at.

Two guys stood with their backs to the bookcase. No one seemed to be hurt. They were already ignoring the books on the floor. Next to them was Hector.

I recognized Rob Wells's voice when he spoke. He was one of the popular guys and didn't usually talk to people as far out of his realm as Hector was. "The thing about American girls," Rob said, "is they expect you to be forward. You should stand really close and touch them when you want to get their attention."

"Yeah," Jeff Savage said. He was Theresa's ex-boyfriend and the fullback on the football team. "Call them five or six times a night to show them you want to be friends."

"Stop by their house unexpectedly a lot," Rob said. "And if a girl calls you a stalker, that means she likes you."

Suddenly this explained a lot about Hector's odd behavior.

I didn't really think about what I did next. As hard as I could, I shoved more books forward. They slammed into the guys with a terrific thud.

I leaned forward onto the now mostly empty shelf. "Did those hit you? I'm so sorry. I get accident-prone when I hear guys telling random people to stalk me."

Rob and Jeff laughed and took off. Hector followed after them, blushing. The librarian came up behind me, her voice a mixture of alarm and anger. "What happened here?"

"Accident," I said. "I think this shelf is unstable."

The librarian was not nearly as gullible as Hector. Not only did I have to pick up the books, I had to go see Mrs. Callahan, the principal. She lectured me about respect for school property, and then gave me after-school detention.

"You're one of the best students in this school," she told me. "I expect more out of you."

That stung.

I missed the rest of world history, so I went to my locker, got my homework, and brooded all through detention. I kept wondering what Trevor would have said to me if I hadn't emptied the bookcase. He'd left the scene of the crime as soon as the librarian had come over to yell at me. Had I ruined my chances with him? I wasn't even sure whether he'd heard the things Rob and Jeff said to Hector. In which case, I'd looked completely psychotic asking him to the dance and then pushing a row of books off the shelf. He probably thought our date would consist of me checking in with my invisible friends and telling him about my past life as a unicorn.

What I didn't worry about was Theresa's reaction to my asking Trevor. Which, looking back, is what I should have thought about.

News travels fast by text.

I don't know exactly when Theresa got ahold of that picture the yearbook staff had taken of me—the one where I stood by the Morgantown High School sign, posing with Lori in our National Honor Society T-shirts. But it wouldn't surprise me if it had been while I sat in detention.

In the photo, I held up a calculus book while Lori wielded a calculator with more buttons than a computer keyboard. Both of us were trying to look ditzy. Visual irony. It's geek humor.

Theresa cropped out Lori and put the picture of me on her blog with lots of brilliant commentary. My favorite was: *Any idiot can hold a calculuss book—and here's the proof!!!!!!!!!!* Of course, it might have been more effective if she'd spelled *calculus* right. Or if she'd used fewer exclamation marks. Really, all of them lined up like that just gave the reader the impression they were about to do the punctuation version of a Rockettes-like dance number.

But I can't blame Theresa for what happened after that. Not even I imagined the photo would go viral or how it would change my life.

CHAPTER 2

The next day I didn't see Trevor until physics class. I expected him to turn around at his desk and talk to me, tell me his answer about the dance. Maybe even rib me about the fall of the Roman Empire books. But he didn't look at me. So was that a no as far as Sadie Hawkins was concerned? Didn't I deserve an official answer? In the mayhem of the library, could he have possibly forgotten that I'd asked him?

When class ended, I leaned over my desk and tapped him with my pencil. "Hey, Trevor," I said, keeping my voice light. "I was too busy flinging books at people yesterday to hear your answer about the dance. Did you want to go or not?"

He scooped his books off the desk, his expression guarded. "Oh, that." For a moment he didn't say anything. Then he gave a really slow "su-u-u-re," as though he might talk himself out of it sometime during the answer.

"Great," I said. I didn't mean it.

Clearly his excitement level about our date ranked somewhere near being swarmed by hungry mosquitoes. And now I was not only going to have to pay for this date, I would have to endure his lack of enthusiasm during it. I smiled at him, said I'd give him the details later, then spent the rest of the day wishing I'd never asked him.

Lori came over that night to cheer me up. She flipped through my closet deciding what I should wear to the dance. "So Trevor has reservations about going—that doesn't mean he doesn't like you. Maybe he's worried that dating will put your friendship in jeopardy."

I sat on my bed watching her and didn't answer. What had put our friendship in jeopardy was his pained answer.

Lori said, "Maybe he's nervous about taking things to the next level."

The next level. As though dating were a computer game.

"Maybe he was hoping someone else would ask him," I said.

Lori reached the end of my closet. She slid the door closed with a thud. "I think you need to go shopping and buy something new. Something really stunning."

"Like that's going to make a difference."

"It will. It's nature's way of attracting a mate. Peacocks have the bright feathers. Fish have the long tails, women have the mall." She made a sweeping motion in my direction. "It's time you wow him with some style."

Which is how I ended up wandering around the mall for the next week, looking for wow. As it turns out, wow is really expensive.

Mostly I was just overwhelmed by all the choices. I didn't know which textures went together or how to accessorize. I'd spent my life wearing blue jeans and T-shirts.

Finally I put together an outfit that didn't cost a lot. I still had to buy dinner, tickets, and pictures. I also splurged on some new stuff to wear to school. I shouldn't have. My college fund was already bleak, but every day that Trevor flirted with me in physics then ignored me at lunch sent me right back to the mall, looking for wow.

Theresa was pointedly nasty to me whenever she saw me, and I'd already found out about the picture she'd put on the Internet. So when the phone rang one afternoon and a professional-sounding woman's voice said, "Hello, may I speak to Alexia Garcia?" I had my suspicions.

"This is she," I said.

"Hello, Alexia, this is Maren Pomeroy, Kari Kingsley's manager."

Right. I knew it was Theresa crank calling. She and the Cliquistas had done this sort of thing before. Theresa had figured out we didn't have caller ID, and that made our house an easy target. Still, I let her go on and waited for the punch line.

The voice said, "I saw a picture of you, and I must say you look uncannily like Kari. I'm calling to see if you would be interested in pursuing a job as her double. But you'll need to keep this strictly confidential—do you think you can do that?"

"Oh, sure," I said. "I'll eat the phone after our conversation so no one will be able to trace the call."

She laughed like she wasn't quite sure how to take my comment and went on. "Kari needs the position filled immediately, and you would have to move out to California, but you'd be well compensated—somewhere between ten and twenty thousand a month. Of course, you'd be required to go through an interview first—"

And the interview no doubt would consist of questions regarding my IQ and if I thought Shakespeare was something a jungle native did before an elephant hunt. Then I would hear laughing in the background and a click.

Instead, I beat her to it. "Theresa, why don't you grow up?" Then I hung up the phone. Some people can be so immature, and I didn't have to deal with that.

I went to the family room and sat down next to Abuela. She wore a plaid housedress and ate Triscuits and guacamole while she watched the end of one of her *telenovelas*. She occasionally shook her head and called out instructions to the characters. "Don't trust him, Consuela! He carries a gun for a reason." Then to me she said, "Never date a man who carries a gun. They're all criminals. Without exception."

"What about policemen?"

She dipped a Triscuit into the guacamole. "They don't make enough money. Who wants to date one of them?"

"I don't know. How cute is this policeman we're talking about?"

She waved the Triscuit at me. "*Teenagers.* All you think about are looks. If you were smart, you would date ugly people. They'll be grateful and treat you better."

Mom says that Abuela is getting opinionated in her old age. Except she isn't that old, and to tell you the truth, I never remember her being anything but opinionated.

In sixth grade when we had grandparents' day at school, the other kids' grandparents came to the classroom to oooh and ahhh over their grandchildren's projects. My grandma ended up cornering Mrs. Hochhalter by the world maps and complaining that schools shouldn't teach that Columbus discovered America. "You can't discover a country if someone is already living on it. That's like me saying I discovered your minivan in the parking lot." Abuela held up one hand. "I discovered it! Give me the keys or I'll give your entire village smallpox!"

My mom came home not long afterward. She worked as the housekeeping supervisor at the Waterfront Place Hotel but also took classes three nights a week to get her business administration degree so she could, in her own words, "finally get a job that doesn't require wearing a polyester uniform." This night she came inside carrying a white garbage bag. Booty from the hotel.

It's not that she stole towels or anything—although we had plenty of those too. When the towels got too old to use, she took them home instead of throwing them away. Ditto for the broken soap bars they couldn't use in the rooms. I'd spent my entire life washing off with soap that had been pieced together.

Antonio, the chef at the restaurant, also kept her supplied with leftovers from conventions and food that would otherwise go to waste—being single and pretty does have its perks in the hotel business.

Mom set stuff on the kitchen table and turned to me.

"Lexi, the school called me about that picture of you—the one where you look like Kari Kingsley."

Technically, I look like Kari Kingsley in all my pictures. I had no idea what she meant. "What?" I asked.

She opened her purse, took out a color copy of the picture, and handed it to me. It was the one where I was wearing my NHS T-shirt by the high school sign, but my hair was blond, and a caption underneath it read "Morgantown High: home of the great thinkers." Someone at school must have copied the picture from Theresa's blog and turned it into a slam of Kari Kingsley and Morgantown High. After all, Kari Kingsley was the patron saint of blond jokes.

"You did this?" Mom asked. "You posed for this picture on purpose?"

"It was supposed to be a yearbook photo."

"It didn't end up in the yearbook," Mom said, her voice tense. "It ended up all over the Internet. Kari Kingsley's manager called the school to complain about them defaming her client. When the school told them it was an actual student in the picture, the manager asked for your name and contact information. The school called to see if I wanted to give it to her." Mom took the picture from my hands. "I had no idea what they were talking about, so I had them e-mail me the picture." She put her hand on her hip. "I can't believe you posed for this right by the school sign. Now anyone who sees this will know where you go to school."

I couldn't muster much fear of Internet predators right then. I had just realized that Kari Kingsley's manager really had called me for a job interview. I sank down onto one of the kitchen chairs with a whimper. "You should have warned me that you gave our phone number to them," I said. "Her manager called, and I thought it was a crank call."

Mom blinked rapidly. "I didn't give her our phone number. I told the school I didn't want her to contact us."

"Well, she got our number somewhere," I said. Which wouldn't have been hard. In such a small town, anyone could have given her my number. "She asked if I'd be interested in a job interview, and"—I put my hand over my eyes—"I hung up on her." This was really not the best way to impress future employers, but if I explained. . . . I looked up at Mom. "Can you get her contact information from the school so we can call her back?"

Mom turned to the cupboard and took plates out. "No. Definitely not."

"She said I'd be paid between ten and twenty thousand dollars a month."

Mom's mouth dropped open. "To do what?"

"Be Kari's double. She didn't say exactly what that was, just that I'd have to move to California. She wants to hire someone immediately."

Mom shook her head and slid the plates into their places on the table. "You can't move to California. You're not done with high school."

"I could work something out with the school." At least I hoped I could. All the zeros in the salary danced around in my mind. "You know how I've said, 'If only I had a dollar for every time someone tells me I look like Kari Kingsley'? Well, I think this would cover it."

Mom let out a grunt and went back to the cupboard for glasses. "Celebrities. They think they can buy anything they want, even people. Well, you're not for sale."

Her reaction didn't make sense to me. "It's a job," I said. "You're supposed to get paid."

Mom put the glasses next to the plates. "Lexi, you don't understand about stars. They're pampered, selfish *tantos*—with egos so big they need extra luggage to carry their self-importance around." Without giving me a chance to say anything, she turned toward Abuela and called out, "Tell your granddaughter it's a bad idea to take money from celebrities. Rock stars, especially, should be avoided like lepers."

I expected Abuela to agree. It had always bothered her that I looked like Kari Kingsley. She would find Kari Kingsley pictures in grocery store tabloids just to complain about them. She especially hated one where some buff shirtless guy draped his arms around Kari. "*Mira esta chica*," Abuela had said with scorn. "Boys see that girl doing those sorts of things, and they'll think our Lexi is no better." Abuela did a lot of head shaking. "Somebody ought to smack that girl good and hard with a Bible."

Leave it to my grandma to use the holy book as a weapon.

But this time, instead of her usual Kari Kingsley com-

mentary, Abuela gave my mother a knowing look. "You had a different view of singers once."

Mom glared at her and jangled the silverware onto the table.

Which made me remember—when Mom was my age, she'd been wild about this country-western band—the Journey Men. She wanted to drop out of school and become a roadie. Seriously. She still had a couple of their posters on the top shelf of her closet. She also had every CD they'd ever made, and I had to endure listening to them whenever Mom felt nostalgic for her high school years.

But what I wanted to do wasn't the same as dropping out of school to become a roadie, because I'd be paid a lot more.

"It's time for dinner," Mom said in that tone parents use to tell you the subject is closed.

I didn't want to let the subject drop, even though I knew it was pointless to argue right then. She was too upset about it—though I didn't understand why. Wouldn't most parents think it was cool to have their daughter make a lot of money doubling for a star? I tried to make sense of her response while we waited for Abuela to pull herself off of the couch and shuffle over to the table.

Probably the thing that upset Mom was the idea of me dropping out of high school and working. College was a sticking point for her. She hadn't gone because she'd been pregnant with me. She'd moved to DC with my aunt, my *tía* Romelia, and gotten a job with a hotel there. She'd spent the last twelve years taking a class here and there, until she was finally at the point where she was almost finished with her degree. She'd always told me to do it the right way. Four years straight through.

But what did it matter if I left high school a few months early or put college off for a year? I'd still get my degree. She should know that.

Abuela sat down at the table. Mom stared at the food and held a fork in her hand, tapping it between her thumb and finger.

Abuela glanced over at her. "Stop worrying, Sabrina."

"Who knows how many people have seen that picture?" Mom said. "Anyone could have seen it."

"Yes, but what are the chances that *he'll* recognize her for who she is?"

Mom didn't answer. She turned to me and said, "Lexi, would you say the prayer?"

I looked back and forth between Mom and Abuela. "Who's *he*?" But as soon as the words left my mouth, I knew the answer. "Oh. You mean my father."

My mother had never told me who my father was. She always said we'd have a talk about it once I graduated from high school and went out on my own. She thought then I'd be mature enough, and if I wanted to contact him, it would be my choice. Which I didn't think was fair. A person should know who her father is all along. I'd grown up feeling like I didn't really know who I was, like a big chunk of me was missing.

Here is the sum total of what I'd been able to squeeze out of my mother in all of my years of trying: My parents met the month before she graduated from high school. He was very handsome—tall, sandy blond hair, blue eyes, and I did look like him, even though I inherited Mom's brown hair and brown eyes. She thought she loved him. They had a very short relationship and were never married. Mom insisted she hadn't kept his identity a secret because he was a convict, a lowlife, or something else that I would be horrified to find out about. She kept his identity a secret because she thought it was for the best.

The only other thing she'd told me about him was that he didn't know I existed.

When I was young, I'd fantasized about him showing up one day out of the blue. I used to imagine him holding the reins of a tawny brown horse with a pale tan mane—a gift for all the years he'd missed in my life. He would smile, excited to meet me. As I grew older, his gifts became other things, but the smile and the dream remained the same. He was out there, looking for me, finally wanting to be a real father. I knew it wasn't true, that it couldn't be true, but still I wanted it.

So I'd heard almost nothing about my father from Mom. Abuela knew things about him too, but she remained surprisingly quiet on the subject. I'd been able to get some information from her because keeping her mouth shut was not her strong point—but Abuela put her own spin on everything, so I wasn't sure how much of it was true.

According to Abuela, my father had money and Mom had contacted him to tell him she was pregnant. She was brushed off, though, told she was a gold digger. Mom decided not to press the matter after that. She had her pride. She would raise me on her own. We didn't need handouts.

Since Mom's and Abuela's stories didn't exactly mesh, I went back and forth as to which I believed. Mostly I wanted to believe that any day a nice man with sandy blond hair and blue eyes would show up with my horse.

I looked at Mom across the dinner table. "Why do you care if my father sees the picture? I thought he didn't know about me."

Mom stopped tapping her fork. "Lexi, please say grace."

"Do I look so much like him that he'd recognize me from a picture?"

Abuela folded her arms and let out a martyred sigh. "I'll say grace. Otherwise we'll starve."

She shut her eyes without waiting to see if Mom and I followed suit. "Our Father, we thank you for this food and ask you to bless it. We also ask you to bless Lexi and keep her far away from those trampy girls who live out in Hollywood, where sin lies like a lion waiting to devour them all. Amen."

I glared at Abuela, but she picked up her fork and ate without paying attention to me. I turned to Mom. "If I worked for Kari Kingsley for a year, I could go to any college I wanted, not just a state university."

Mom pushed rice pilaf around on her plate. "There's nothing wrong with going to a state university, and besides, if you needed the money for college that badly, I would track down your father and ask him for it. But you can make it on your own. What you don't get in a scholarship, we can finance. You're bright and talented, and you don't need to take money from people who'll treat you like a second-class citizen. You're better than that."

"You don't know that Kari Kingsley would treat me that way," I said.

Mom gave me a half grunt, half laugh. And okay, I admit she had dealt with a few celebrities when she worked at an upscale hotel in DC. I used to love hearing her stories about them. The singer who insisted on having rose petals put in her toilet every morning. The actress who wanted someone to spray her brand of perfume around her room before she checked in.

But still.

I held out my hands to Mom. "Ten to twenty *thousand* dollars a month. I can put up with a celebrity for a few months for that much money."

"Your self-respect shouldn't have a price tag."

I opened my mouth to protest, but she held up one hand to stop me. "Your school gave me this Maren Pomeroy's contact information. I'll e-mail her tonight and tell her you're not interested. That way we won't have to worry about her calling again."

I simply stared at Mom. How could she be so unreasonable about this?

She ignored my stare and continued to push food around on her plate. "Larry and I are going out tonight. We're going to a chamber orchestra performance." And just like that, our discussion was over.

Larry worked as an accountant for the hotel and was about as much fun as a ledger full of numbers. He insisted on taking Mom to things in which she had no interest whatsoever, and for a reason I never fully understood, this did not bother her.

I didn't comment, though, because I was not speaking to her. Ever again.

"Orchestra." Abuela repeated the word like it had a bad taste. "You should go dancing. What's wrong with this man that he doesn't know how to dance? He's *aburrido*." Boring.

Mom let out a grunt. "I've had my share of flashy, romantic men. It never works out. Stable is good. Boring is even better." Mom took a sip of water. "Boring men hardly ever dump their girlfriends. It takes too much effort. Plus, they make good fathers because they have no outside hobbies."

I didn't want to even think about the possibility of Larry being my father.

I pushed away from the table, walked to my bedroom, and slammed the door. Then I threw myself down on my bed. I didn't have a headboard, footboard, or the canopy bed I'd always wanted when I was little. I looked at the dresser that Mom had picked up at a garage sale, and my closet filled with clothes I'd bought at thrift shops and clearance sales. All of it came into sharp focus.

I'd never held it against Mom that I didn't have a big house like my friends or that we didn't take expensive vacations like their families. Mom couldn't afford to buy me a car, let alone one like Theresa and the Cliquistas' fleet of sports cars.

And then there were the little things—how I always had to pretend that I didn't like movie theater popcorn when I went out with my friends because I couldn't afford the ticket *and* the junk food—how I never had the latest or the nicest of anything. But this? This wasn't fair.

I thought about her statement that if I really needed money she would ask my father for it. Had she not noticed the way we'd lived for the last eighteen years?

Eventually the doorbell rang. I heard Larry's and Mom's voices out in the living room and then a couple minutes later Mom opened my door.

"I'm leaving now. Make sure Abuela doesn't get into trouble while I'm gone."

I knew she wanted me to laugh. I didn't even look at her.

"Look, I'm sorry you're disappointed about the job, but trust me about this, Lexi. It isn't right for you."

She shut the door, and I thought about my summer jobs at McDonald's. Apparently those were right for me. I was a flipping-burgers type of girl.

But I didn't want to be anymore.

CHAPTER 3

Mom had to be to work by seven A.M., so she was always gone before I got up, but just to torture myself I read her e-mail to Kari's manager. It said, "Ms. Pomeroy, Alexia appreciates your offer, but we feel she needs to stay here and finish school."

Which I suppose was better than writing, "I'm sorry but we think celebrities are such jerks that we'd rather spend our time using cast-off towels and piecing together broken soap than ever work for you."

In physics Trevor was acting weird. He kept leaning toward my desk like he wanted to talk to me, but then he never said anything.

After the third time he did this, I leaned toward him. "Is everything okay?"

"Yeah," he said as though he didn't know why I asked. Then after another moment, he added, "I was thinking we should talk about the dance."

"Okay." I had never discussed the details with him, and suddenly I looked forward to that. It would seem more official, less awkward when we were deciding the restaurant and who we'd go with. Lori had finally asked someone.

"I'll talk to you after school, all right?"

"Sure." I didn't say more. The teacher had sent a glare in our direction.

I was actually in a good mood for the rest of school. For once I would have Trevor's attention all to myself. No teachers to squelch our conversations, no Theresa to distract him.

After my last class, I waited at my locker, putting my homework into my backpack extra slowly. He didn't show up. I stayed a while longer, scanning the hallways. He should have been more specific about where he wanted to meet.

When I still didn't see him, I walked to his locker. He wasn't there either. Had he forgotten?

I told myself not to be disappointed and headed toward the school door. He probably meant he'd call me after school.

As I walked through the lobby, I saw Trevor and Theresa standing together by the trophy case. Kissing.

I stopped walking.

Well, this was nice. I walked over to them, arms folded, and cleared my throat. "So, Trevor, you wanted to talk to me?"

Trevor lifted his head. "Oh," he said as though just remembering I existed. "Alexia."

Theresa slid her arm around his waist. A triumphant smile spread across her face. "Sorry, but he's going to the dance with me."

I kept my eyes on him. "Has anyone ever told you that you have a lot of class?"

He didn't answer, didn't move away from Theresa.

"No? Well, there's probably a good reason for that." I turned and walked out the school doors, without waiting to see if he ever came up with anything to say. My throat felt tight, and my stomach lurched with each step I took.

Stupid dance. Why had I even bought tickets? What was I going to do with them now? And if Trevor didn't want to go with me, why hadn't he just said so in the first place?

It didn't matter, really. He and Theresa were both pigs.

I walked faster. I wanted to run. I wanted to sprint all the way home and lock myself in my room and cry. I was probably going to cry anyway, but I wouldn't let myself run. He wasn't worth it.

Guys just couldn't be trusted. Didn't I already know that? Wasn't that the first thing I'd learned in life, that men wouldn't be there for you?

And now I was crying, and I wasn't even home. I brushed a streak of tears off my cheek and forced myself to think about something else. The ugly yellow paint of the house I passed. The weeds growing in the sidewalk cracks. The big black car behind me, which was obviously lost because it was driving really slow.

I pushed myself to go faster. What was wrong with me, anyway? Had I misinterpreted Trevor's flirting? Was I just his second choice if Theresa didn't work out?

I took deep breaths. The black car behind me still drove so slowly that it didn't pass by. And then I realized what I should have known all along. It was following me.

So apparently Trevor had come after me but still didn't have the courage to speak to me. I stopped walking, turned around, and waited for the car to catch up to me. Jerk. I would tell him exactly what he could do with his apology.

But the driver's tinted window slid down to reveal a woman, probably in her early thirties. She looked like a newscaster. Shoulder-length dark hair, perfectly set, tons of makeup. She smiled over at me. "Hi, I'm Maren Pomeroy, Kari Kingsley's manager. Can we talk for a moment?"

I didn't move. In fact, the whole thing sort of freaked me out. The woman who worked for Kari Kingsley? Why was she here when she'd said she lived in California?

Ms. Pomeroy kept smiling at me. "We can go to your house, or perhaps you'd like to go to a restaurant and get something to eat?"

I took a step away from the car. "Sorry, but I don't think my mother would like that. I mean, bringing a stranger to the house." I took another step down the sidewalk. "Or, you know, going someplace without asking her."

The back door swung open, and for a moment I expected some guy in a trench coat to step out and grab me. I was on the balls of my feet, ready to sprint away. And then I saw Kari Kingsley sitting in the backseat. She wore a pair of tight jeans, red spiky heels, and a red halter top underneath a loosely crocheted white sweater. She took a pair of sunglasses from her eyes and slid them onto her head with apparent irritation.

"I've spent a long time on a plane to come see you. The least you could do is give me ten minutes of your time."

I gaped at her. I couldn't help it. As though she might not have known it, I said, "You're Kari Kingsley."

"Yeah." She slipped her sunglasses back on. "Do you want to get in the car before your little school friends come by? I didn't plan on causing a scene."

"Oh. Sorry." I slid into the car, put my backpack on the floor, and shut the door. I did it without even thinking about it. It was like the president of the United States had asked me to get in the car. No wonder my mother resented celebrities. You just felt compelled to do their bidding.

As soon as I shut the door, Ms. Pomeroy pulled away from the curb. "A restaurant or your house?"

"Only say your house if you've got something five star to eat," Kari said. "I'm hungry."

Actually, we probably did have something good to eat, but I said, "Restaurant." I wasn't about to bring Kari Kingsley to my run-down house or introduce her to my grandmother—seeing as the last thing Abuela had said about Kari was that she should be hit with a Bible.

Kari took her glasses off again to better survey me. I stared back at her, comparing each of her features to my own. Her nose was sharper than mine, her lips a little thinner. But the tilt of our eyes, the rise of our cheekbones, even the slope of our chins were the same. I'd seen her picture a hundred times, but it was still surreal to see my face on a stranger; like gazing into a mirror—well . . . a sophisticated blond mirror.

"So do you look this way naturally?" she asked. "Or did you go to a plastic surgeon and tell him to put my face on yours?"

I nearly laughed at the image that painted—me strolling into a plastic surgeon and picking out lips and cheekbones like they were ingredients on a pizza. "It's all natural."

She leaned back in her seat, shaking her head. "Sheesh, you look more like me than I do."

I didn't think that was possible, but I didn't challenge her on it.

"I actually have brown hair," she said. "My mom was Mexican."

I liked her more right then. Even though her life had been nothing like mine, we had something in common.

"So is my mom," I said. "*¿Hablas español?*"

She shook her head. "My mom died when I was baby, and my dad," she gave a dismissive shrug, "he only knows enough Spanish to give instructions to the cleaning ladies. It sort of ticks me off now that it's chic to be Latina."

"Really, it's chic now? I must have missed that announcement."

Kari laughed and then glanced out the window at the row of small houses we passed. "You've lived here too long. In California nobody cares what color you are so long as you're beautiful."

"Oh. Well, that's a much better system." I was being sarcastic, but I'm not sure Kari picked up on this. She nodded as though she agreed with me.

From the front seat Ms. Pomeroy said, "Kari, why don't we go back to the hotel. That way you can order room service and talk privately."

The hotel. Oh, no. I knew as soon as she said it that we'd go to the Waterfront Place, where my mom worked. It was the nicest hotel in Morgantown.

My stomach clenched. I wasn't even sure what worried me more, the fact that my mom might see me walk in with Ms. Pomeroy and Kari Kingsley after she'd already turned down their job offer, or the fact that I might have to introduce Ms. Pomeroy and Kari Kingsley to my mom while she wore her housekeeping uniform.

I knew without them having to tell me that they had come to reoffer the job. They didn't have another reason to be here.

"Actually, there are some good restaurants in Morgantown," I said.

Kari waved off my suggestion with a set of immaculate red nails. "We shouldn't be seen together in public. Maren told you this has to be kept secret, right?"

Before I could answer, Ms. Pomeroy said, "I told her." Her eyes found mine in the rearview mirror. "You haven't told anyone about this except for your parents, have you?"

"No," I said.

"Good," Kari said with a sigh. "Really, I shouldn't have even come, but I wanted to judge you for myself. Not that I don't trust Maren's opinion, it's just that—"

"Flying out here gave you an excuse to abandon the studio," Ms. Pomeroy added dryly.

Kari smiled. "Exactly. And now I'm satisfied." Her gaze ran over me. "With a few changes, you could pass for me."

I fidgeted with the edge of my seat. "You got the e-mail from my mom where she turned you down, right?"

Kari brushed off my words. "We got it, but you can always finish high school online, you know. We'll get you a tutor if you need one." She tilted her head, considering me. "Although Maren tells me you're brilliant. You even belong to the smart club."

"National Honor Society," I said.

"Well, there you have it." She lifted a hand in my direction. "That's one of the reasons why I need you so much."

"Need me to do what, exactly?" I asked.

"I need you to pretend to be me at some functions."

I laughed. I thought she was joking, and I waited for her to tell me what she really wanted me to do. Only she didn't.

When I'd thought about what being a double meant, I'd imagined, vaguely, that I would be used as a decoy to throw off the paparazzi when she went to events or stuff like that. Like a stunt double. Not once did I ever think she actually wanted me to pretend to be her.

"I can't do that," I said.

"Why not?"

I leaned toward her, shaking my head. "We don't look so much alike that we're interchangeable."

She let out a sigh and wrinkled her nose. "Yeah, I need to talk to you about that. We'll have to change your hair, and you'll need to start wearing makeup."

"I do wear makeup," I said defensively. "Just not very much."

Kari's gaze ran up and down me again. "And definitely your clothes have to go . . . oh, and your walk too. We watched you come out of the school, and there's no good way to tell you this, but you looked like you were plowing through a snowdrift." She held out her hand, palm up, as though showing me something. "You need some finesse. You know, some strut."

"I don't always walk like that," I said. "I've had a bad day."

From the front seat, Ms. Pomeroy called out cheerfully, "We're at the hotel. Let's finish talking about this upstairs."

I looked out the window. Yep, it was my mom's hotel, which meant not only did I have to worry about bumping into her, but also all the employees who knew me. I gripped the door handle and told myself I should tell Ms. Pomeroy and Kari that my answer was no now, before I got into trouble with my mom. I knew I couldn't accept her offer.

But I didn't. I don't know whether it was curiosity, or whether I was still starstruck at being invited to come up to Kari's room, or whether a small part of me hoped I'd find a way to make the job work.

I could earn between a hundred and twenty and two hundred and forty *thousand* dollars a year. I couldn't even imagine everything I could do with that much money.

Kari slipped her sunglasses on and pulled a hoodie over her head. "The room is in Maren's name," she said, "so hopefully no one will recognize me." Kari took another pair of sunglasses from her purse and handed them to me. "Here, as long as you're walking around with my face and those clothes, you'd better wear these."

I'd had her face for my entire life and at times wore a lot worse than the jeans and T-shirt I had on, but I didn't argue with her.

Kari peered around the parking lot, then sighed before opening the door. "Sometimes it's so hard to be me."

I followed her out of the car but didn't tell her that actually *I* had a better chance of being recognized at the hotel.

We walked quickly through the lobby, and I kept my head down. We went to the elevator and Ms. Pomeroy pushed the up button. So far so good. Kari was busy telling me that in California I'd stay in Ms. Pomeroy's guest room and have my own driver and the use of other professional staff.

Why did elevators take so long?

Jonathan, one of the waiters from the hotel restaurant, walked past us with a dining cart on his way to the service elevator. I wanted to turn so he couldn't see my face, but Kari was still talking.

Just as our elevator door opened, he glanced over. His

eyes widened with surprise when he saw me. "Hey," he called over, "how ya doing?"

Kari flung her hand up like a traffic cop. "I'm sorry, but we don't have time to talk to fans."

And then she grabbed hold of my arm and propelled me into the elevator.

Well, that was probably going to be hard to explain to Jonathan later.

Ms. Pomeroy pushed the eleventh-floor button, and Kari leaned against the wall and let out a sigh. "That's the thing I hate about this business. People never leave you alone. They think they have the right to talk to you whenever they feel like it." She gazed at me with a solemn expression. "You're going to have to learn how to deal with the public as part of your job. You can't be nice to people or you'll be mobbed. You have to cut them off and walk away."

Ms. Pomeroy nodded. "We'll try to protect you as much as possible."

The elevator opened and we stepped out. Alleen, one of the maids, walked by carrying an armful of towels. She did a double take when she saw me, then smiled. "Hey, there, what are you doing here?"

Kari shook her head and increased her pace. "Look, we're very busy and don't have time for autographs."

Alleen's eyebrows shot up at that, but I didn't have a chance to explain.

Great. There was no way my mom wouldn't hear about this.

A few moments later, we walked into one of the luxury suites. The high ceiling, large sitting room, and flowing curtains made it seem more like a high-end apartment than a hotel room. The smell of room freshener and clean sheets surrounded me.

Kari took her sunglasses and jacket off and tossed them on the coffee table, then sank down into the couch. I sat down on the love seat and placed my sunglasses next to hers. Ms. Pomeroy picked up the room service menu and rattled off food choices until we chose something. Then she picked up the phone and ordered.

Kari said, "Tell them to hurry. I'm starving." She leaned toward me confidentially. "And despite the *National Enquirer* putting me on anorexia watch, I'm not one of those celebrities who think starving is a good thing."

Into the phone Ms. Pomeroy said, "Can you bring that as fast as possible? We'll give you an extra tip."

I wondered if Ms. Pomeroy always did everything Kari asked. It just seemed odd to me, an adult taking orders from someone wearing a halter top.

When Ms. Pomeroy finished with the phone, she sat down on the couch next to Kari, and they both looked over at me. "Well, then, we'd better get on with the interview. You'd be willing to change your clothes and hair, wear makeup, and work on your walk and mannerisms?" Before I could answer, she turned to Kari. "Is there anything else you think Alexia needs to change?"

Kari nodded. "Her voice. She needs to lose the hillbilly accent."

"I don't have a hillbilly accent," I said.

Ms. Pomeroy pursed her lips as though considering it. "Your *a*'s are a little too long, but besides that, your voices are similar enough that I don't see any reason this won't work."

"Neither do I," Kari said. "We'll see how well you can pull off being me for a couple of easy events. If you can do it, you'll have the job for the year."

Which still didn't make sense to me. I said, "Changing my hair and makeup won't fool people who know you."

Kari relaxed into the couch cushions, looking elegantly at home against the rich fabric. "I'm not asking you to fool my friends or staff. But you could pass for me with everyone else. And they're the only ones I need to fool because they're the ones who pay to see me."

"You mean like at concerts?" I couldn't, even for a moment, imagine myself up in front of a stadium full of people.

"Not big concerts. I'm talking about smaller stuff, mall openings, parades, maybe lip-synching a few songs for some state fairs and rodeos." Before I could say anything else, she went on. "They pay me forty thousand dollars a pop, and I need the money too much to turn them down. I've got some debts that are bleeding me dry, but I don't have the time to do that stuff. That's why I need you to do it."

"Isn't that illegal?" I asked.

Kari rolled her eyes. "That's why you're keeping it a *secret.*"

Ms. Pomeroy leaned forward, smiling at me like I was silly for asking. "Celebrities use doubles all of the time, and lip-synching is just part of the business." I must not have looked convinced. She added, "Think of it as a win-win situation. People want Kari to make appearances. It helps them with fund-raisers, membership drives, getting people to come to their events, that sort of thing—but she doesn't have the time. She's got to work on her next album. If you go in her place, the groups are happy, Kari still gets things done, and you get paid four thousand dollars an event, five if it requires travel."

I looked at my hands. Unlike Kari's immaculate fingernails, mine had been chewed down to nothing. It was one more difference between us that she'd overlooked.

"They don't really care about me anyway," Kari said. "All I am is an image. If they believe they're getting the real thing, they'll be just as thrilled."

"We'll help you so you'll be ready," Ms. Pomeroy added. "And you'll get a new wardrobe, a hairstylist, a professional makeup artist, and a driver—what more could you want?"

For a moment I imagined myself on stage, the spotlight washing over me, thousands of people screaming and clapping.

But even as the applause echoed in my mind, I knew I

wouldn't do it. If I didn't mess up and get caught—and that seemed like a risky if—wasn't it still wrong to get paid to trick people? I couldn't imagine proposing the idea to Mom. I let the calculations of money drain from my mind in a drizzle of dollar signs. "I'm sorry. My mother is not going to let me do this."

Kari stared at me as though I'd told her the world was flat after all, but Ms. Pomeroy didn't lose her smile. "Well, you're eighteen, aren't you? You're old enough to make your own decisions."

"I'll think about it," I said, because I was too polite to say "I know, and I just made my decision."

When my mother heard about this, she would gloat about the fact that I had sided with her in the end.

"What's there to think about?" Ms. Pomeroy said. "If going against your mother's wishes would create a financial hardship on you, I could add another five hundred dollars per presentation." Her smile had an edge to it now. "I don't think you'll ever find a better job than this. You'll make more than most professionals. And you're going to have to cut the apron strings from your mother sooner or later."

"It's not about the money," I said.

Ms. Pomeroy arched an eyebrow, waiting to hear what it was about.

"There's a difference between cutting apron strings and cutting ties," I said. "I'd like to still be welcome at my house for Thanksgiving dinner."

Ms. Pomeroy didn't blink. "Five thousand in state. Six thousand out, and you can have Thanksgiving dinner at my house. I'll throw in Christmas too, if you want."

She was serious. Which is why I stared at her open-mouthed.

Kari turned to Ms. Pomeroy. "Don't force her into it. She doesn't want to ruin things with her mother. I can understand that."

Ms. Pomeroy let out a sigh and fluttered one hand in the air as though brushing away the subject. "Fine. We came all this way, but if you've decided you'd rather do the events yourself, I won't stop you." Her voice changed just enough to alter her meaning. "After all, you're fine out in the public eye."

Kari glared at her, then turned her attention back to me. "That's the other reason I hoped you'd do this for me." She ran her fingers across the hem of her shirt, twisting it. "I've never really liked crowds—"

"You don't like crowds?" I repeated. It seemed contradictory—rock stars were supposed to want crowds of people to come to their concerts.

"I love singing, performing, doing the stuff that's scripted—but crowds are a bunch of people watching you, and taking pictures of you, and just waiting for you to mess up so they can laugh at you. I've said a couple things that were blown way out of proportion, and everyone made fun of me and now I . . ." She wiped her hands against her jeans. "I freeze up when reporters point cameras at me. I don't want to be in front of people for a while. But you're so smart, you wouldn't have to worry about saying the wrong thing."

And then I felt bad because I'd made fun of her when I'd seen those clips too. Not once had I ever wondered how it had affected her or how hard it must be to mess up in front of the entire world.

I said, "Everyone says the wrong thing sometimes. It doesn't mean you're not smart."

A knock sounded on the door. Ms. Pomeroy stood up, but Kari was closer. "There's the food." As she walked toward the door, she added, "Thank goodness they're fast."

That *had* been fast. For a moment I worried that when Kari opened the door it would actually be my mother, her hands on her hips, chewing me out in Spanish, like she did whenever she was angry.

But it wasn't. When the door swung open, Don, one of the older waiters, stood behind a dining cart. "Your Caesar salad, fettuccine Alfredo, and bacon cheeseburger, well done."

"Thanks." Kari pulled the cart into the room and then went to shut the door.

Don held out a clipboard and a pen to her. "If I could get you to sign this—"

Kari huffed out an exasperated sigh and put one hand on her hip. "Don't you people know when to stop? Really, there are times to leave celebrities alone, and this is one of them."

She shut the door with a thud.

"Kari," Ms. Pomeroy said, getting to her feet again, "he was asking you to sign for the food."

A blush spread across Kari's face. "Oh."

The knock came at the door again.

This time Ms. Pomeroy opened it. Don still stood there, clipboard held out in his hand. She took it from him and scrawled a signature on the paper while Kari took her fettuccine Alfredo off the cart. Kari cast Don another glance. "You should have told me you needed my signature *for the food.*"

"Sorry, miss." He looked over at me while Ms. Pomeroy handed him the clipboard back. His eyebrows rose when he saw me, but he didn't say anything else.

Ms. Pomeroy shut the door and brought my plate to me. I wished I hadn't ordered anything. I didn't want to stay here with them after I'd already told them no, and my resolve was slipping. I could see why Kari didn't want to be in front of reporters who could broadcast every mistake she made to millions of viewers.

As Kari handed me my cheeseburger, I said, "Isn't there some other way you could make money? You know, maybe some product endorsements?"

Ms. Pomeroy took the lid off her salad and sifted through it with her fork. "Kari actually lost a product endorsement after her MTV awards speech. What she needs is to get her next CD out, and that won't happen unless she has time to work on it."

Kari cut into her pasta and her voice took on a bitter tone. "My father could help me, but he won't."

Something else we had in common, apparently. That same sentence had run through my mind during my mother's talk about college expenses. "Why not?" I asked.

"We're not really on speaking terms. Mostly because he doesn't speak, he lectures." She shrugged as though it didn't matter, but the tenseness didn't leave her face. "He doesn't like my spending habits, but I don't see why he cares so much. He doesn't need the money. He actually turns down product endorsements."

I picked a french fry off my plate and nibbled at it. "Your father gets asked to do endorsements? Because he's your father?"

Ms. Pomeroy leaned toward me like a teacher explaining directions on a test. "Kari's father is Alex Kingsley."

Even though she'd said it in a way that indicated I should know him, I didn't.

She added, "The lead singer of The Journey Men."

"Oh, The Journey Men," I said. "We have all their CDs. My mother is a big fan."

As soon as the words left my mouth, something clicked into place in my mind. No, actually that isn't the right word. It wasn't a click, it was a push—the push of a row of dominoes, each falling into another, tumbling, dropping, scattering until everything was a mess.

Kari took a forkful of fettuccine, then glanced over at me

and didn't eat it. "Are you all right? You've gone completely white."

"I'm okay," I lied. I could be wrong. I mean, what were the chances? I tried to picture the CD covers of The Journey Men and the posters I'd seen in my mother's closet. The lead singer—he had sandy blond hair, but what color were his eyes . . . ?

"Which one is your father?" I asked, and my voice came out almost normal. "Is he the tall one with sandy blond hair and blue eyes?"

"Right," Kari said. "That's him. Usually front and center."

I stared back at her without blinking. The last domino had hit the ground.

CHAPTER 4

My heart pounded so hard I could hear nothing else. I had to get away. I couldn't look at Kari. I stood up, leaving my plate on the coffee table. For a moment I felt dizzy; my voice sounded detached, even to me. "I think I'm going to talk to my mother about this whole thing. Maybe we can work something out."

Ms. Pomeroy saw me heading to the front door and called, "You can step into my bedroom to use the phone."

I shook my head. I wasn't having this conversation over a phone, not when my mother was somewhere in the hotel. "I'll be right back," I said.

I'm sure Kari wouldn't have approved of my walk as I went down the hallway. It had no finesse, no strut, just a lot of resentment.

The elevator took me to the basement. I marched down the hall to the housekeeping office. I half expected Mom to not be there. She spends a lot of time checking the rooms, but when I went through the door, I saw her standing by her desk, talking with Don. The whir of the washing machines and dryers muted but didn't cover their words.

"I'm positive," he said. "She was in the room with that ditzy singer—the one who looks like her."

"Kari Kingsley," I said. "Her name is Kari Kingsley."

They turned and saw me. My anger must have been evident. Mom said to Don, "I'll talk with you later," and he left.

I stared at her, emotion biting into the back of my throat. "Alex Kingsley is my father, isn't he?"

The color drained from my mother's face. She sank into her chair.

I always thought I'd be happy when I found out my father's identity, but instead I churned with a rage I didn't understand. "I can't believe you didn't tell me," I said. "You knew Kari and I looked alike because she was my sister, and you never told me."

Mom's eyes registered shock. "She knows? She told you?"

And that hurt too—that Mom admitted the truth so easily now, when I'd never been able to pry it out of her before. I was not about to answer her question.

Tears pushed against my eyes. "All this time, we had pictures of him in the house," I said. "I thought you hadn't shown me any pictures because you didn't have them. I thought it would be hard to track him down. But I saw him and heard him all the time, and I didn't even know it!"

"Lexi—" she said, but I didn't let her finish.

"Don't call me Lexi!" I yelled. "You named me Alexia. You named me after him, didn't you? How could you do that? You gave me his name and then made sure I had nothing else from him—not knowing who he was, not even knowing what he looked like. You could have just pointed him out on the CD covers."

She had always known how badly I wanted to know what my father looked like. Every time I dreamed about him finding me and couldn't picture his face—every time I scanned a crowd and saw a blue-eyed man with sandy blond hair, I had wondered about him and felt empty inside.

"Does he know anything about me?" I asked. "I want the truth this time. All of it."

She let out a ragged breath, then looked away. I thought she wouldn't answer, but she did—in a voice so calm I knew she'd rehearsed this speech. "When I was your age, I was obsessed with Alex Kingsley—you knew that already. He came to a concert in Charleston the end of my senior year, and I drove there to see him. He picked me out of the crowd and pulled me up on stage with him. Then when the song ended, he asked if I'd wait backstage for him. I already felt like we were destined to be together, and this was proof I was right."

Her gaze flickered back to mine, and she shook her head. "I loved him so much, and when you feel that way, your mind stops thinking. I know you can't understand this. You've always been so sensible, but I wasn't like you that way. I was headstrong, impulsive."

I'd never thought of my mother as being impulsive. She went to work every day and to class three nights a week. She did the dishes, paid the bills, and hardly ever lost her temper. I couldn't imagine her even being my age, let alone my age and starstruck.

"Alex said he'd picked me out of the crowd because I looked so much like his late wife. She'd died eight months before from a brain aneurysm. Kari had only been a year old when it happened, just a baby. Alex was out on the road at the time and blamed himself for not being there. He could have gotten her to the hospital in time if he'd been home. We talked a lot after the concert, and he told me things he'd never told another person. I believed him about that; I don't think it was just a line he used. He was hurting, and I wanted to make him feel better so badly."

She kept her gaze on the desk. "I gave him my phone number, and he said he'd call me, but he never did, which stung. I was still thinking about our destiny together. In my mind I could see myself stepping in and being a mother for his daughter, that's how crazy in love I was. I didn't realize then that celebrities only care about people who are as rich and famous as they are."

She pushed out a breath, and her gaze finally returned to me. "I also didn't realize I was going to be the mother of his daughter after all. When I found out I was pregnant, I tried to call him. I got as far as his manager. I told him why I needed to talk to Alex, and he called me a gold digger and"—she paused and lowered her voice—"a few less flattering things. He told me to leave Alex alone and hung up on me. So the truth is, I never knew whether Alex found out or not."

"Why didn't you keep trying to reach him?" I asked. "You could have demanded a DNA test or something."

She shook her head. "Your *abuela* wanted to hide my pregnancy, wanted to make sure no one found out." Mom stopped for a moment, as though mentally correcting herself. "Well, it wasn't just Abuela. I didn't want everyone from school to know. That isn't the sort of thing you announce at your graduation party. If I'd demanded a paternity test, it would have been in the tabloids. Besides, I didn't want to take his money if he didn't care anything about me."

So it had been because of her pride. Hadn't she ever thought I needed a father, that at least he deserved the chance to be one?

As though Mom had been able to read my mind, she said, "You have to understand, I adored him before I ever met him—that's blind love, and it's easy to get crushed when you have that kind of love. A daughter's love for her superstar father—that would be blind love too. If I had told you he was your father and he rejected you the same way he rejected me—I didn't want you to get hurt. I wanted you to have a firm sense of who you were, to be grounded before you met him, so no matter how it turned out, you wouldn't be devastated."

I wouldn't listen to her words; I wouldn't let them soak in. "You should have told me," I said. "I shouldn't have had to find out like this."

"I didn't mean for this to happen. If I had known Kari Kingsley would show up here . . ." My mother gripped the edge of the desk, clenching it. "Does she know? Is that why she's here?"

"No, she doesn't know. She's here to convince me to take the job, and I'm going to."

The words made something in Mom's expression change. She snapped back to being herself. "You can't just drop everything and run off to California."

"Yes I can." I turned and headed toward the door. "I guess I'm more impulsive than you thought."

My mother followed, switching into Spanish. "*Te tratarán como suciedad.*" They'll treat you like dirt. "Is that what you want? Is the money worth your dignity? If it is, we might as well get a lawyer and just ask for back child support."

"This isn't about the money," I said. "This is about me finally figuring out the other half of me—the half you've always kept a secret."

She took hold of my arm, stopping me as I reached the hallway. "You don't need to go anywhere to figure out who you are. You're Alexia Garcia: a beautiful, smart, talented girl. Can't you see that?"

I pulled my arm away from her. "You don't understand this." She couldn't. She'd always known both of her parents. She hadn't grown up half empty.

"I understand—you're doing this because you're mad at me. It's a bad reason, Lexi." She reached out again but didn't touch my arm. "Think about it before you get caught up with these people."

"Why should I, when you didn't?" I turned and walked

away from her, but I could feel her watching my every step.

I went to the service elevator, stood inside shaking, and stared at the buttons.

Despite the scene with my mother, I didn't know what to do. I didn't even know what to say to Kari. Did I tell her she was my half sister? What exactly was the proper etiquette for announcing that sort of thing? It had been a huge shock to me, and I'd had at least a little forewarning. I'd always known I had a father somewhere, and I might have brothers or sisters. But how would Kari take the news about what her father had done? How would she feel about a sister—about *me* being her sister?

I looked down at my worn tennis shoes and their fraying laces, at my faded jeans, and my nondescript T-shirt. I compared them to her outfit, right down to her cosmopolitan red heels and flashy gold earrings. I was glad she didn't know who I was, and I wasn't going to break the news to her. Not now. Not until I'd talked to Alex Kingsley. Alex Kingsley—that's who he was to me. I couldn't call him my father, not even in my mind.

I imagined myself telling him. I saw his face now, where before there had only been a blurry guy standing beside a horse.

Was it possible he would be happy, that he'd want to be some sort of father to me?

But, then again, if he hadn't cared enough about my

mother to even call her, why would he care about me? Maybe he'd call me a gold digger too. I didn't know anything about him or how he'd react.

I leaned against the elevator wall. Maybe my mom was right and it was better to have a lawyer contact him and ask for a DNA test. Only, getting a lawyer seemed like mounting an attack against him. If he felt attacked, I'd lose the chance to ever have a real relationship with him.

I pictured meeting him at some posh lawyer's office. My mom and I would drive there in our beat-up Taurus with a three-inch crack in the windshield and a side mirror that had been superglued back into place after Abuela had knocked it off while backing out of the garage.

He'd be so impressed with us.

It was better to do it my way.

I pushed the button for the eleventh floor and in a couple of minutes stood outside of Kari's door. I took a lot of deep breaths before I knocked. Ms. Pomeroy answered. I walked in and forced a smile.

Kari had finished her meal and was sprawled out on the couch with a *People* magazine. I looked at her profile, taking in our similarities again. It was so obvious now that we were related, a truth standing there in plain sight—no, not standing, waving its arms around, jumping up and down. Why hadn't I figured it out the first time I saw her on a CD cover?

I knew I was staring, so I turned my gaze to Ms. Pomeroy. I kept my voice even and told myself they had no reason to suspect anything. Sometimes strangers look alike. "I'll take the job on one condition. I want to meet Alex Kingsley."

Ms. Pomeroy raised an eyebrow. "Why?"

"I already told you I was a fan. We have all his CDs."

Kari laid the magazine on her stomach and craned her head around to look at me. "So when it was about meeting me and making a lot of money, the answer was no, but when there's a chance to meet my father, the answer is yes?"

I shrugged. "I've wanted to meet him since I was a little girl."

She picked up the magazine too quickly, and the pages rustled in protest. "Well, I feel special now."

Ms. Pomeroy walked to a desk and picked up a briefcase. "I'm sure a meeting can be arranged—after you've done a few events for Kari. Let's get started on the paperwork, shall we? You'll be listed as an assistant. No need to tell anyone more about your duties." She pulled out a paper and handed it to me. "Here's a nondisclosure form. This means you can't talk to the tabloids about Kari at all. No interviews, no pictures, no leaks, no book deals, or anything along those lines. We're clear about that?"

"Absolutely," I said. In fact, I wanted the press to find out about this less than Kari and Ms. Pomeroy put together.

For the next few minutes, I sat at the desk and filled out every piece of paper Ms. Pomeroy handed me.

She watched my pen moving across the paper. "You'll

need to learn how to write Kari's signature to sign auto-graphs," she said. "Beyond that, don't write anything for anyone while you're pretending to be her. Your handwriting is nothing like hers."

I nodded. "When am I leaving for California? Tomorrow? Tonight?"

She laughed at my eagerness. "We can give you time to pack, tie up loose ends, withdraw from school—"

I slid the last piece of paper back to her. "Don't. If you give me time I'll probably change my mind."

For a moment her gaze zeroed in on me, calculating, then she picked up the papers and straightened them into a pile. "Your mother still doesn't approve? You did tell her you were going, didn't you?"

"She knows I'm going. She just doesn't think I should."

Ms. Pomeroy slipped the papers back into her briefcase. "And what does your father think?"

That was the question, wasn't it? Yesterday, an hour ago, I would have shrugged, like I'd done a thousand times, and told her my mother was single. I couldn't bring those words to my lips now.

"My father doesn't live with us." My voice sounded tense, wrong somehow. And I could see her making note of that, like she made note of everything.

She nodded, closed her briefcase, and stood up. Before she walked away, I asked, "Do you know Alex Kingsley?"

"I used to work for him before I became Kari's manager."

"What's he like?"

Ms. Pomeroy glanced over at Kari to see if she was listening. She wasn't. She'd moved on to a *Glamour* magazine.

"I think very highly of him." The tone of her voice hinted at more than professional admiration. "When Kari's next album comes out, I'll probably go back to working for him." She smiled not so much at me, but at the thought of him. "I won't have any trouble arranging a meeting for you."

I should have been glad that she had such easy access to him, but instead my skin prickled. It was stupid to feel jealous on my mom's behalf just because she'd kept Alex Kingsley's posters. And still listened to his CDs. Sometimes incessantly. Until I had to retreat to my room and block out his voice by blasting my own music. Mom had moved on with her life. Still, I looked at Ms. Pomeroy's flawless makeup, her perfectly outlined maroon lips, and wondered if she'd ever kissed my father. I didn't like the thought.

• • •

Ms. Pomeroy drove me to my house so I could pack a few things. I should have invited her in. It would have been the polite thing, but I didn't. She knew my father. Maybe she'd been to his house. Somehow I couldn't stand the thought of her looking down on our cramped living room and sagging couch. I didn't want her making judgments on the kind of life my mother had been able to provide.

Instead I got out of the car and asked Ms. Pomeroy to pick me up in a half hour. That would be all the time I needed to throw a few belongings into a duffel bag and say good-bye to Abuela.

I figured I wouldn't tell Abuela I was leaving until the last possible moment. That way she wouldn't try to lecture me.

But as soon as I went into my bedroom, she appeared in the doorway, wearing one of her ever-present housedresses and smelling like homemade fry bread. "You're really going?" she asked. "You're going to chase after that man just like your mother did?"

I should have anticipated that Mom would have called her. I shoved socks and pajamas into the duffel bag. "I have a father and a sister. Don't you think I have a right to know them?"

"You have a mother and grandmother who raised you." Abuela's voice cracked. "Don't we have a right to you too, Lexi?"

I looked up to see tears rim her eyes and then spill over. I'd never seen Abuela cry. I stood frozen for a second, stunned by the change. She thought I was abandoning her, that I wouldn't come back. I went and threw my arms around her. "It's okay," I said. "I won't stay away long. I'll go to college, just like we've always planned."

She hugged me, her body all the types of softness her words never had been. "Get it over with and come home," she said. "Come back before they change you."

"No one's going to change me," I said. "I'll always be your granddaughter worth her weight in trouble."

She held me for a moment longer, then stepped away. "You remember, when you put yourself above others, you also cut yourself off from them. Cut off. That's what death is."

I didn't know what she meant by that, but I was busy packing, and besides, you just didn't want to ask Abuela to elaborate. "Nothing bad is going to happen to me," I said.

I wasn't thinking clearly, I knew. I was bound to forget things I needed. I wished I had an actual suitcase, because suddenly there were so many things I wanted to take. Silly things. The shells I'd gotten from the Chesapeake, where my mother and I had gone on vacation. A cheap stuffed bear an old boyfriend had won at the state fair. The picture on top of my dresser of Lori and me sitting on Santa's lap. We'd been at the mall, and Lori thought it would be funny to get a picture, so we'd stood in line with a bunch of pre-schoolers for an hour. Every one of these possessions said "I love you."

I didn't have room for any of them.

While I went between my room and the bathroom gathering things, Abuela gave more instructions. "Eat three meals a day. Real meals. None of those Californian supermodel meals. They don't eat actual food, just puffed air. Make sure you call us every day. Remember to say your prayers. And don't start running around with boys. All the boys in California are gangsters. Or movie producers. And those are even worse."

When I'd finished packing, I looked out the living room window. Ms. Pomeroy's black sedan waited out front.

I gave Abuela another hug. "I've got to go. You take care of Mom and make sure she stays out of trouble."

She held on to me, patting my back. "You remember who you are, Lexi."

"I will." I knew that's what she wanted to hear. But I thought, How can I remember what I never knew?

I went outside without looking back. The screen door clanked a good-bye, and then I climbed into the sedan.

We drove back to the hotel, picked up Kari, and went to the airport. Ms. Pomeroy apparently had taken what I'd said about changing my mind to heart and didn't give me time to reconsider. When we pulled into the airport, a private jet waited for us.

Ms. Pomeroy took my duffel bag as we climbed on the plane. "We'll go shopping tomorrow to get you what you need. Clothes, shoes, makeup." She gave me an appraising scan. "Fingernails."

Even though I'd been the one to suggest leaving right away, and even though Ms. Pomeroy was all smiles and promises about what a great job this would be, I didn't trust her.

It was the missing words. It was the fact that I knew responsible adults: my mother, my teachers—responsible adults followed a certain script. Any of them would have told me to think carefully about choices that would affect my life. Any of them would have said I shouldn't rush through this decision. I had waited for Ms. Pomeroy to say these things and I'd formed answers in my defense. But she didn't question my reasons at all.

Which is why I had no doubt that she'd just as easily toss me aside if things didn't work out.

CHAPTER 5

I'd never ridden on a plane before, let alone a private jet. It would take me to a new state, a new life, one where I would get to know my sister and father. I should have been blissfully happy, but as I sank into the soft leather seat, all I could think about were the good-byes I hadn't said to my friends and the one I had said to my mother.

When would I see them again? I felt a sharp pang of regret for leaving this way, but it was too late to change my mind now. The engine had started, and the plane was rolling toward the runway.

Once we were airborne, Maren—she told me not to call her Ms. Pomeroy—began my training. Basically I was immersed in all things Kari Kingsley for the duration of the flight. Maren had me practice copying Kari's autograph about four hundred times until my *K*'s stood straight up and my *A*'s were round. Then I watched music videos and taped concerts of Kari.

While she danced, she always wore sequined outfits and glitter covered her body and hair. Glitter was her trademark. Her first album was called *All That Glitters Isn't Gold: Some of It's Diamonds,* and her first hit had been entitled "Glitter Girl." So she'd been sparkly ever since. I stared at the crowds cheering for her on the screen, then glanced over at her sitting in the seat not far from me.

She was casually flipping through magazines. It struck me all over again that Kari was a rock star. And my sister.

Every once in a while, she looked over at the tapes and chimed in with commentary. "That was the concert when some guy got past security and flung himself on the stage. Totally threw me off. I think celebrities should be allowed to Taser certain fans."

And: "That video lasted three minutes but took two full days to film."

I didn't doubt it. She changed hairstyles in the video eight times.

And: "The heels on those boots don't look that high, but you should try doing side lunges in them and keeping your balance."

Which made me nervous. "I'm not going to have to, am I?"

Maren waved a hand in dismissal. "You'll just be doing a few basic moves as you lip-synch. Nothing hard."

But I wasn't sure I believed her. Maren had a smooth voice, like the kind that used-car salesmen on TV always had.

"You need to get a feel for how she moves and how she talks," Maren told me. "Do you see how erect her posture is? That's from years of dancing. You'll need to walk the same way." She looked me over with only a small amount of discouragement visible in her expression. "Have you ever taken a dance class?"

"Yes." Actually, I'd taken a lot of dancing and singing lessons. Mom had never had a great salary, but she always found someone willing to trade classes for housecleaning. All those lessons I hadn't asked for suddenly made sense. Ditto for the musicals at school Mom forced me to be in. She must have figured I'd inherited my father's talents, and she wanted me to develop them.

Now that I thought about her sacrifice, I felt bad that I didn't have a passion for either of those things. I was happier reading or playing sports.

"Your dance instructor will help you learn a few simple routines," Maren said. "I'm hiring new staff for you so they won't realize you're not Kari. You'll need to make sure you keep up the act all the time. Alexia is gone now."

I thought of Abuela's words—to remember who I was—but I nodded at Maren anyway.

After the plane landed, a limo met us on the tarmac and drove us to Beverly Hills. I stared out the window, taking in every house, tree, and bush we passed. It was stupid, but I couldn't help myself. I almost expected to see Brad Pitt out watering his grass or something.

I'd never been one of those starstruck teenagers who had posters of buff actors or who followed stars' blogs. True, I did buy a magazine once because it had a picture of Grant Delray—a twenty-one-year-old rock sensation—on the cover, and maybe I kept the magazine on my bookshelf so I could look at his picture every once in a while, but that didn't make me a fanatic.

That was just the normal, red-blooded-girl reaction to sky blue eyes and perfect features.

Being in California where the movie stars lived, I couldn't help but look for them.

The limo dropped us off at Kari's gated mansion. Maren had her BMW parked there, so the two of us switched cars. As I did, I gaped at the fountain by the circular drive, the columns, and the balcony. No wonder Kari was in debt. How much room did one person need?

Before Kari went inside, she turned back to me with a smile. "I'll see you later—you know, either at Maren's or in the mirror."

"Kari will be by in a few days with some of her clothes from last season," Maren said, as though reminding Kari of this fact.

"Oh, right," Kari said. "I have a ton of stuff to give you."

I opened my mouth to thank her, but she added, "Last season I was ten pounds heavier, so it should fit you fine."

"Thanks," I said, but the word lacked something in sincerity. She didn't seem to notice.

We drove to Maren's house, a three-story town house overlooking Santa Monica and decorated like a model home. The fabric on her curtains matched the throw pillows on her couch, which matched the covers on her dining room chairs. Vases and candlesticks and bowls with bamboo shoots growing in them had been placed artistically around the room. I was afraid to touch any of it.

Even though it was practically the middle of the night in

West Virginia, I knew I wouldn't be able to sleep. Sitting on the satiny blue bedspread in the guest room, which matched the dust ruffle, the curtains, and the guest bathroom towels, I felt impossibly far away from home. I wanted to hear my mother's voice again.

I took my cell phone out of my duffel bag. I'd turned it off after our fight, but I saw she'd called six times. I dialed home, and Mom picked it up halfway through the first ring. "Lexi?"

At the sound of her voice, my words caught in my throat. "I'm sorry I yelled at you, Mom."

"I know, honey. I'm sorry too. Where are you?"

"I'm in California—at Maren's house."

There was a pause, then, "You're already there?"

"I told you I was taking the job."

Her voice spiraled upward. "You didn't say you were leaving right away."

"I had to. Otherwise, I knew I'd change my mind."

"If you knew you'd change your mind, then you knew it was the wrong choice." She said something else after that, but I didn't hear what. Abuela was throwing in her two cents in the background.

"Tell Abuela everything will be fine. I'll only stay long enough to get to know Kari and to meet my father."

Mom said, "What about finishing high school?"

"Maren said she'd get me a laptop with wireless Internet. Can you call the school and ask them if I can turn in assignments long distance?"

"I'll call them," Mom said. Then she said something to Abuela in a hushed tone. Abuela doesn't speak in hushed tones, though, so I heard her say, "What does she think she's going to find with her new family anyway?"

Mom said, "I want you to check in with me every day—you'll do that?"

In the background Abuela was still giving her opinion. "Nothing good ever came from a musician! Except music. *That's* what she's going to find."

"Yes, Mom, but I've got to go," I told her. "Let me know what the school says."

She sighed and said she'd call them in the morning, and we said our good-byes.

My stomach stopped clenching after I'd talked to her, but I still felt odd—disconnected. Like my life had started in one book and suddenly I'd found myself in a completely different story.

I'm just doing this long enough to meet my father, I told myself again—then I'll go home. But when I shut my eyes to go to sleep, all I could see was Kari's signature, repeating under my eyelids over and over.

• • •

In the morning, Maren—still resembling a news anchor, even though she wore jeans and a beige sweater—took me to a beauty salon. Once there, Peter, a Hungarian hairstylist, ran his fingers through my hair while he shook his head and made disappointed grunting sounds. My current hairstyle was apparently a tragedy.

He spent the rest of the morning transforming my "limp brown mop into radiant blond tresses"—his words, not mine. This involved not only bleaching and highlighting it, but adding permanent hair extensions, a process that felt a bit like mice were burrowing through my skull. After that was done, a manicurist gave me acrylic nails and then a makeup artist introduced me to foundation, bronzing powder, liquid eyeliner, and a bunch of stuff that required little brushes.

Once they spun me around to face the mirror, I was shocked. For a second, I didn't recognize myself. Kari Kingsley stared back at me. But not the Kari I'd seen in the tabloids and the interviews on TV. I was the Kari from her album covers and press releases. I looked like the touched-up version of her, where her features were softer.

I had to touch my face to make sure it was really me. And then I laughed. It was so odd to think that I could have looked like this all along.

After that, I washed my face off and they made me apply the makeup again to see if I could do it myself. A makeup artist would still do my face for public events, but I had to learn how to do it for everyday wear. It took me three times to get the eye shadow right. There was enough blending, shadowing, and contouring involved that it should have required an art degree.

While the salon beautified me, Maren set up a bank account to deposit my paychecks into. She gave me a credit card with Kari's name and a copy of Kari's driver's license so I could buy whatever I wanted.

A wardrobe was the next thing on our to-do list. The shopping trip was also, as Maren put it, my first public test to see if I could pass for Kari. I was more than a little nervous about it, and as we drove to the boutique, I said, "What if someone sees me, snaps my picture, and it ends up on the front of a magazine? People who know Kari will figure out I'm an imposter."

Maren flicked a piece of lint off her sweater. "First of all, that's why you'll wear your sunglasses anytime you're out. Second, pictures vary, even taken of the same person at the same event. Kari's friends would just assume the picture was a little off. Third, the big magazines have photo shoots for their covers, and tabloids usually run pictures of celebrities who do something interesting—so don't shave your head, lose or gain a lot of weight, get divorced, or have another celebrity's baby. Do you think you can manage that while we're out today?"

I nodded.

"If someone takes your picture, at worst it will end up on the Internet with the other hundreds of pictures people took of celebrities this week. Nothing to worry about."

I leaned back in my seat, trying to appear as at ease as Maren was.

"I've hired a bodyguard," she said as we neared the store. "Nikolay is waiting for us at the boutique. You needn't worry about making small talk with him because his English is limited. Still, he has excellent references. He's ex-KGB."

"The Russian secret police?"

"Right." She smiled like this was a good thing, but it only made me more nervous. I couldn't shake images of some burly guy interrogating people in dimly lit rooms.

When we pulled up, I recognized him right away. It would have been hard to miss the six-foot-three-inch guy in a gray suit who stood guarding a parking spot for us. The car stopped, and he opened the door for me. He didn't smile, just scanned the street as I got out. Then he followed Maren and me inside, stood against one wall, and scrutinized the store.

It was a shop that Kari didn't usually frequent, so the staff didn't know her. As we walked toward the clothes, Maren whispered, "Stand up straight, shoulders back, and show a little superstar attitude."

Superstar attitude, I told myself. I'm not Alexia. I'm Kari Kingsley. I sparkle when I'm onstage. The salesclerk, a woman toting more jewelry on one arm than I'd ever worn on my entire body, smiled and told me what a fan she was then brought over clothes for my consideration.

I did okay being Kari. All right, I admit that I gasped the first time the salesclerk handed me a shirt and I saw the price tag dangling from the sleeve. For two hundred and fifty dollars, Tommy Hilfiger himself had better come to my house and iron it. But after that, I stopped gaping at the price tags and pretended it was normal to try on a pair of eight-hundred-dollar shoes.

I put on things that I never would have tried back home. They were too bright, too flashy, and yet when I looked in the mirror they worked. I saw Kari's body and not my own. I stared at myself, turning side to side, while the clerks hovered by the dressing room telling me how chic and beautiful I looked. I did feel beautiful—and not the sort of beautiful your mother tells you that you are when she's cheering you up. I felt powerfully beautiful, like I could walk out the door, swish my hair around, and the world would give me whatever I wanted.

This was Kari's normal life—this attention, this pampering. And I could have had it all along if I'd grown up as Alex Kingsley's daughter.

It was a thought I hadn't expected to have, not with such resentful force anyway, but it wouldn't leave, and seemed to get stronger every time I posed in front of the mirror.

I could have lived here in California, and no one would have ever sneered at me because I was poor. I would have grown up with Kari, had famous friends, been given all sorts of things—who knows, maybe I would have been a rock star too.

The feeling grew and swelled until I didn't want to play this charade just to get to know Kari, meet my father, and then go back to West Virginia. I wanted to know what it would feel like to live a Beverly Hills life. Maybe it wasn't too late to have it. Maybe this person in the mirror with a thousand-dollar outfit hugging my figure was the real me.

As soon as this idea came to me, I remembered Abuela's instructions not to change who I was. I had said I wouldn't, but that might be impossible. I'd been changed the moment I'd left West Virginia. Now I had to figure out who exactly I was changing into.

While Maren took my clothes up to the register, a teenage girl came into the store with her friend. She watched me for a minute, then walked up. "Excuse me, you're Kari Kingsley?"

She sounded like she didn't believe it. Of course she didn't—I looked wrong. I walked wrong. I couldn't possibly pull this off. But the next moment she laughed nervously like she knew she'd asked a stupid question. "I loved your last album. 'Two Hearts Apart' is my favorite song." She thrust a pen and a piece of notebook paper at me. "Can I have your autograph?"

"Sure," I said, with more gratitude than Kari would have shown. The girl had given me a great compliment, though: I could pass for Kari Kingsley.

I signed the paper and then signed the credit card slip with a flourish. Both times my *K*'s were perfect.

Shortly thereafter, Maren ruined my good mood. As we got into the car, she handed me the clothes bags and said, "There. These should hold you over until we can get you down to the next size."

"What?" I asked.

Her gaze traveled over me, and she shrugged. "The camera adds ten pounds."

"You think I'm too fat?" All right, I admit I have a weakness for Almond Joys, but I was not overweight. Any high-calorie food I ate was counteracted by the fact that I had to walk everywhere I went, including the mile to and from school.

Maren pulled out into traffic without glancing at me again. "Don't complain. It won't be hard. I've already hired a personal trainer for you."

. . .

As it turns out, the sentences "It won't be hard" and "I've hired a personal trainer for you" are contradictory. There is nothing easy about a personal trainer. Right from my first session with Lars, every muscle in my body hurt. Muscles I didn't even know I had hurt. Blinking took effort. And I was not cheered up by the grapefruit halves Maren gave me for snacks or her words of encouragement: "No pain, no gain. Get used to it."

She also made me practice walking in front of mirrors for hours.

"Shoulders back. More confidence. Don't walk—*glide*!" she'd yell at me while I attempted to duplicate Kari's smooth strut in heels that were so high they should have been outlawed. It never looked right.

But then, I bet even Kari herself couldn't glide while every muscle in her body ached.

Maren coached me on sounding like Kari and public speaking. The most annoying part of this involved her ringing a bell every time I said the word "um." I'm not sure whether this actually decreased the times I said "um," but it certainly increased my desire to stomp on the bell.

I had to memorize hundreds of details about Kari. She was a vegetarian, so I couldn't eat meat. She was a role model to young girls, so I couldn't swear or drink alcohol. She and her on-again, off-again boyfriend, Michael Jung, a star on the soap *Where Angels Dare*, were taking a break from each other right now. So although I could flirt with guys, I couldn't overdo it.

Maren scheduled me for an hour-long dance lesson every day and then increased the time to two hours, which I resented. Really, I am a good dancer, despite what Jacqueline (pronounced *Zhak-lean*), my private dance instructor, says. Granted, when Maren hired her and told her she'd be teaching routines to Kari Kingsley, maybe Jacqueline expected me to have more experience, but she kept shaking her head as though horribly disappointed. "Where is jour energy? Snap zose moves! Do jou think people want to see zat on MTV?"

It was like taking dance lessons from a drill sergeant.

Basically, Maren controlled my schedule from the time I woke up in the morning at six until I went to my room at ten P.M., exhausted. I had to practically sneak my phone calls to Lori in between training sessions. I told Lori I'd come to California because I'd located my dad and sister, but didn't give her any more details. She gave me updates about everyone in school, including Trevor and Theresa. They were still dating but I'd stopped caring.

If I was on the phone for more than a few minutes, Maren would stand in front of me tapping her wristwatch until I got off. And despite what she said before about letting me finish my schoolwork online, she hardly gave me any time to do it. More than once I fell asleep facedown in my world history book.

"The key to any celebrity's success," Maren told me if I was less than enthusiastic about what she had planned for me, "is a firm schedule and hard work." Then she'd add some backhanded insult like, "I'm sorry those things weren't emphasized in your life before, but really, it's time you thought of bettering yourself."

I had to memorize the lyrics to Kari's songs, and if I messed up while I lip-synched them, Maren would put her hand over her eyes like I'd given her a headache and say, "Didn't you ever listen to the radio back in West Virginia? I thought *everyone* knew these lyrics."

The only thing she ever complimented me on was the way I'd incorporated so many of Kari's mannerisms. I hadn't, of course. They were my mannerisms too.

Day after day I worked through the mundane details of turning myself into Kari. I didn't tell my mom about most of it. I knew she wouldn't approve of me deceiving people. She already sighed a lot every time I called her. She wasn't happy that I left home, so I was more than a little surprised when she sent me her sapphire necklace.

My mom had only had one really nice thing her entire life: a sapphire pendant surrounded by diamonds on a gold chain. She'd never told me where she'd gotten it, but I knew it had sentimental value to her—otherwise she would have sold it long ago to pay bills.

I don't ever remember seeing her wear it. It always sat in her jewelry box, reigning over the lesser rings and necklaces she wore day to day. Once when I was little, I took it out to play with and got in huge trouble, but Mom always told me that when I was older it would be mine.

When I found it there, nestled in a clear jewelry case next to my books, I held it in my hand, watching the light blink blue off its surface. I couldn't believe she had sent it. Then I saw the letter explaining everything.

Dear Lexi,

Your father gave me this on the night we met. He purchased a piece of jewelry for his wife every time he went out on tour, and he'd bought this piece for her during the tour he was on when she died. He couldn't bring himself to return it or to sell it; he couldn't even take it out of his guitar case. It stayed there for months, causing him pain every time he pulled out his guitar and saw it.

Since I resembled her so much, he said he knew it would look good on me, and he made a present of it. I took it because I wanted to help him find a way to heal, to get past the agonizing reminders.

I only wore it that night. I've always felt it didn't really belong to me, but it should belong to you now. If Alex doesn't believe who you are, show it to him. Even if he doesn't remember me, I'm sure he'll remember it.

Love,

Mom

I put the necklace back in its box, a sick feeling of disappointment rattling around in my chest. I'd always loved that sapphire. It seemed like something a queen would own. I had looked forward to wearing it someday, maybe my wedding day. Now I didn't even want to keep it. It should be Kari's, not mine. Alex Kingsley had bought it for her mother, the woman he'd loved—not my mother, the woman he'd discarded.

So it sat in its box on the dresser reminding me every time I saw it that I'd started out life second best.

Sometimes when I was supposed to be doing my homework, I would type Alex Kingsley's name into an Internet search. I must have seen a hundred pictures of him from different events, mostly old, but some new ones too: With a starlet on his arm at the Grammys, being inducted into the Country Music Hall of Fame, as a national spokesman for abused and neglected children. I found that one ironic. I wondered what people would think if they knew he had a daughter he'd neglected to take care of her whole life.

A few times Maren caught me looking at his website, but she never said anything about it. She just raised an eyebrow, gave me a pointed look, then walked away.

I found myself wondering incessantly whether Alex Kingsley's manager had told him my mother was pregnant. Sometimes I thought my father had known about me all along. Then I felt a rage so strong it blocked out every other emotion.

I even wrote a letter to him. I poured out every angry thought onto the paper. "You don't deserve to know anything about me," I said. "I won't show you my baby pictures or home videos, or tell you about myself. I will never sing for you."

But maybe he wouldn't care. Maybe he'd write a check to cover back child support and tell me not to bother him again.

I deleted the letter so Maren couldn't accidentally find it. But it remained in my heart. I could have repeated it word for word.

Then, other times, I was convinced Alex Kingsley's manager hadn't told him anything about me. In those moments I trembled with hope and fear. Anything could happen. He could love me.

Maren said she would take me to a benefit concert he was doing on May 13, nearly two months away. Since she had been Alex's assistant before she came to work for Kari, it would be easy enough for her to come up with an excuse to take me along backstage to see him. She would introduce me as Kari's body double for an upcoming music video.

I wasn't exactly sure how to segue that into a longer conversation with him, and I daydreamed different scenarios.

Sometimes I slipped him a note telling him I needed to talk to him. Sometimes I said it out loud. Sometimes I dreamed that he took one look at me and knew who I was.

That scenario wasn't likely, but still I liked to think about it.

I would probably just hand him a note with my home phone number written on it and say, "You're about nineteen years overdue to talk to Sabrina Garcia. You might want to make the call this time."

CHAPTER 6

I saw frustratingly little of Kari during my training, and I never got to see her without Maren carefully observing everything I said. It made it hard to have any sisterly bonding time. So one day I convinced Maren that I needed to observe Kari directly, to make sure I had everything down before my first public debut.

Maren drove me down to the recording studio so I could see what went on during a session. She told me that when Kari was finished, we could both go back to Kari's house so I could study her firsthand. It was a bigger deal than I'd imagined. Before we arrived, Maren made Kari's bodyguard and personal assistant clear anyone with a camera out of the parking lot. Maren didn't want to clue in anyone from the press that she had a Kari double with her.

She phoned ahead and told Kari's staff and the music technicians that I was an actress working on a movie about Kari's life, but even then, I wore no makeup and had my hair pulled up in a baseball cap so I looked as little like her as possible. We didn't want the staff to put two and two together when I started doing events for Kari.

"Her driver will take both of you back to her house when she's done recording," Maren said as we walked into the studio. "Don't let Kari do anything stupid."

"Like what?"

"Like going out together in public." After a moment's thought, she added, "Also no skinny-dipping where paparazzi might be present, no driving to Vegas, and no going online to try and refurnish her house with antiques from Italy. Returning stuff overseas is awful."

We walked to the control room, and Maren spoke to Kari's assistant for a few minutes, then left to run errands.

I stood among half a dozen people watching Kari through a large window. Kari's staff pretty much left me alone. Every once in a while, her bodyguard sent stony glances in my direction, but he did that to everyone, so I didn't take it personally. Kari stood in the recording room, earphones on, swaying to the music as she sang into the mike.

I'd heard her songs on the radio, but it was still odd to see her creating one. It made it seem more real, more amazing. She had a beautiful voice, deeper and richer than mine.

I wondered for the hundredth time what it would have been like to grow up knowing we were sisters. I imagined Kari and me on camping trips, at amusement parks, running through waves at the beach, with our arms flung around each other making silly faces for the camera. She would have given me fashion tips and told me how to act around guys.

Instead of those memories, all I had was an empty aching spot. I wanted to somehow make up for everything I'd missed out on even though I knew it was impossible.

After a couple hours of Kari singing and stopping and

changing backup singers, and rewriting parts, and then resinging parts, she decided to call it a day. The tech guys weren't happy about this. Apparently she hadn't made any progress.

It didn't matter. Kari took off her headphones and walked into the control room unapologetically. Even in jeans and T-shirt, she was all flash and confidence. She dismissed her staff, telling them she was going out with me, then nodded in my direction. "You ready to ditch this place?"

I glanced at the clock. I'd heard Maren tell Kari more than once that she needed to get this album done. She was supposed to debut some of her new songs at a mega concert in San Diego on May 6. "Won't Maren be mad if you leave now?"

Kari rolled her eyes and grabbed her purse. "I'm not making this album for Maren. I'm making it for my fans, and they'll be a lot madder if it's garbage." She put on her sunglasses, then walked out of the door and motioned for me to follow. "You can't beat a dead horse," she said over her shoulder, "and I've not only beat this one, I've dragged it through eight octaves and a chorus. At this point, the dead horse could sing better."

"That's not true." I hurried to catch up with her. "You have a great voice."

I had thought a driver was taking us to her house, but there was no sign of one. She walked to a silver Porsche, took out her keys, and unlocked it. "I've got a good voice, but you can find good voices in every high school chorus and church choir. I want to be a good songwriter too. It takes real talent to write hits. Not many singers can do that."

"You've done it before."

She opened the door and slid inside. "My dad helped me write the songs on my last CDs."

"Oh." I got into the passenger side, casually letting my hand run across the seat. I had to. I wanted to know what a Porsche felt like.

"I wrote most of my hit songs," she said, and started the car. "My dad would just come along and change a chord. Add a bridge or something. Redo a few lyrics."

"Well, I'm sure he'd help you again if you asked."

"I'm not asking him." She checked for traffic, then pulled out of the parking lot, going too fast. "I can do this by myself, and I'll prove that to him and everybody else. I don't want to live underneath his shadow anymore." Her expression was terse for a few moments, looking ahead fiercely. Then she sighed and slid me a glance. "Sorry for snapping at you. It's just . . . you have no idea what it's like to grow up with a dad everybody loves and thinks is perfect."

Well, she was right about that.

"I can write hits," she said. "I just need some inspiration. Songs never come when you're under stress. They come when you're having fun, when you're in sync with life . . ." She paused for a moment considering her own words, then switched lanes. "Which is why I've decided that instead of going to my house so you can study me like some sort of science project, we should go do something fun."

"Okay," I said, a little nervous about what that might mean. "But we can't go out in public together, or go skinny dipping, drive to Vegas, or buy Italian home décor. Maren's orders."

Kari took her gaze from the road long enough to give me a conciliatory smile. "I bet it's a ton of fun living with Maren. Does she give you a schedule and a whole list of rules to follow every day?"

I sat up straighter. "She said I had to because that's how you lived."

Kari snorted. "That's how she *wants* me to live. The woman has no concept of what an artist's life is like." She switched lanes again and slowed for a light. "Luckily she has the hots for my dad, so she never gets too mad about anything I do. She wants to stay on my good side."

I'd been right. My stomach twisted. I'm not sure why. I knew Alex Kingsley had dated lots of women, but I didn't want him to ever date Maren. She was so cold and judgmental. How could he like her when he hadn't been interested in my mother, who was warm, funny, caring, and whose beauty came not in the form of practiced poise, but was just there naturally?

I kept my voice even. "So are they an item?"

"Not yet. Dad doesn't have a clue, and I'm not about to tell him. If she gets in good with him, then she'll stop working for me altogether."

My expression must have shown I wasn't happy. Kari looked at me and said, "Sorry she's such a downer. Now I bet you wish she had a crush on your dad."

Unfortunately she already did. The light changed, and we moved forward. I asked, "So what did you want to do to have fun?"

She pursed her lips, thinking. "We could go find some drunk guys—just show up and start talking to them. They'd think they lost their minds seeing two Kari Kingsleys in front of them."

I laughed, but shook my head. "No. We're not going to torment drunks."

She thought for another moment. "You speak Spanish. We could fly to a small South American country where no one knows who I am and be tourists."

"Kari, you have a huge following in South America. You've sold a million CDs in Argentina alone."

"Really?" She glanced over at me. "How do you know that?"

"Maren makes me memorize those kinds of facts because I'm supposed to know everything you know."

"Oh. Then it's ironic I didn't know that." She let out an amused laugh, but I didn't join in. Long hours of being quizzed on Kari trivia will suck the humor right out of you. She tapped her thumbs on the steering wheel. "What do you usually do for fun?"

"I used to hang out at the mall or see a movie with my friends. Sometimes we'd go to a school game and then go to Dairy Queen." It sounded low class, but I'd been trapped in dance studios and fitness rooms for too long. I missed my old life more than I thought I would.

"I can't do any of that stuff," Kari said. "I'd be trampled by fans." She said this wistfully, as though she'd like to be anonymous for a while.

I stopped being jealous of her right then—well, a little bit anyway. What must it be like to not be able to hang out in public places?

"Let's go horseback riding," she said. "I've got some great horses, and the stable is really good about working with celebrities. I call them up and tell them I'm coming with a guest, and they get everything ready for me. No questions, no leaks to the paparazzi."

I perked up in my seat. "Horseback riding sounds way better than hunting down drunk guys or fleeing from fans in South America."

We drove to the stable where two of Kari's horses were boarded. As we went through the private entrance, Kari told me that she actually had three horses. Her third, a gelding named Chance, lived at her dad's ranch in Hidden Valley. Chance had been a gift from him to Kari when she turned twelve years old. And—unbelievably—he was tawny brown.

When she told me this, I snapped right back into jealous mode and came close to doing something psychotic like kicking a random bale of hay and yelling, "I can't believe he gave you my horse! You got a dad at your birthday and a horse!" But I didn't. Chalk one up for self-control.

I climbed onto this huge black horse and hoped he was gentler than he looked. Kari gave me a crash course in riding and then we followed a trail into the nearby hills. Wearing helmets and sunglasses, and with our hair pulled back into ponytails, we weren't recognizable. We might have been any two sisters out for a ride.

Kari talked about her album and its frustrations. She didn't want the studio to Auto-Tune her because if her fans were used to hearing songs that were perfected digitally, then her live performances would always suffer by comparison. She'd have to lip-synch them just to sound right. She also said a bunch of stuff about stylization in lieu of enunciation, and vibrato, and other stuff I didn't understand. The girl might not have known when Saint Patrick's Day was, but she knew a ton about music.

Finally Kari said, "Sorry for dumping that on you. I was supposed to let you ask questions about the music business and stuff. So what do you want to know?"

I had a lot of questions, but none of them were about the music business. Even though Kari had said it was hard to grow up with a father everybody loved and thought was perfect, I had a hard time convincing myself that those were bad things. Unless it was all image and no truth. "What was it like growing up with Alex Kingsley as your father?"

Kari held the reins loosely, her posture casual enough that I could tell she was comfortable on a horse. "He stayed pretty busy with recording and touring. I traveled with him a lot when I was little, so I pretty much grew up on tour buses. I didn't know any differently—I thought every kid had an entire band sing them to sleep at night."

This still didn't tell me what type of person he was, so I tried again. "Did he help you with your homework and teach you to ride a bike and stuff?"

Kari cocked her head at me. "Maren told you to ask that question, didn't she? She wants me to feel guilty so I'll call and make up with him. Well, I'm not doing it, so tell her to forget it." Kari snapped her reins and her horse picked up speed, but she still spoke loud enough over her shoulder for me to hear. "Remind Maren that he also volunteered to play at my prom so he could keep an eye on me—thus ruining prom night and embarrassing me in front of my friends." She sent me a pointed look. "Also, the last time I asked him for a loan, he said that he wasn't a bank. My own dad. So I'm not calling him. I'm not seeing him."

I urged my horse to go faster in order to catch up with her, too absorbed with what she said to worry about getting jostled in the saddle. I could see her point about prom night, but still, he seemed really nice. I tucked that knowledge away with both the pain and the pleasure it brought me.

"We don't have to talk about your dad if you don't want to," I said when I rode by her side again. "We'll talk about you." I should ask something normal, like how she decided which fans to give autographs to when a line of them were waving pens at her, or what she did when she was waiting to go onstage, but I kept wondering how she would react when she found out I was her sister. Would she be excited, or would she see me as an encroacher? Maybe she'd hate me. "Did you mind being an only child?" I asked. "Did you ever want a brother or a sister?"

She turned to me, surprised, and laughed.

"What?" I said, afraid she'd somehow guessed my reasons for asking.

"It's just a weird question. No one has ever asked that before. But sure, I guess when I was little, I wanted somebody to play with. As I got older, I realized brothers and sisters are a pain, though, and who wants that?" Her gaze returned to me. "Admit it, I bet there've been times you wished you were an only child."

"I *am* an only child," I said, and then wondered if I should have said it. It wasn't quite true.

"Really?" She let out a huff of disbelief. "It's wild how much we have in common."

Which was the understatement of the year.

"Do you sing?" she asked.

"I've done some musicals at school."

"Have you ever had a boyfriend named Michael?"

"Nope."

"Good. Stay away from those. They're nothing but trouble."

I laughed, and she went on asking questions about my

life, looking for more similarities. They weren't hard to find. We both loved swimming, and hated jogging. We loved comedies and romances, hated horror movies, sad endings, or anything where the dog dies. Loved hot chocolate—really, anything that was chocolate—but hated the taste of coffee. It made me wonder how much of a role genetics plays in everything. I also wondered if our places had been switched if I would have ended up with her personality and she would have ended up with mine. Maybe she would have been the one in the National Honor Society and I would have been on YouTube insisting that animals were people too.

With every question she asked, with every exclamation of something like, "I love Chinese food too!" I almost expected her to figure the truth out for herself. We looked so much alike, and she already knew that my mother had been an Alex Kingsley fan.

She didn't guess, though, and I couldn't bring myself to tell her. Not before I had a chance to meet with Alex Kingsley himself. Besides, while only I knew the secret, I felt powerful. I could watch Kari and learn stuff about my father—and neither could hurt me. Not really. Once they knew, the power would be in their hands. I wasn't sure which reaction I feared most—outright distaste or frozen, horrified silence.

Finally, when she ran out of questions, I said, "Well, there is still one big difference between us. We both grew up only children, but I always wanted a sister."

I hoped she remembered that when she found out the truth.

• • •

After two and a half weeks of dancing, learning to glide in high heels, and memorizing Kari facts with more fervency than I'd studied for the SAT, Maren decided I was ready for my first real event. I was going to a club opening. Kari had been invited by the owner—was actually getting paid to show up there opening night—but since the owner had never met Kari, Maren thought it was the perfect place to test me out before I started the mall openings/rodeo concerts/parades she had lined up.

Kari was only grudgingly letting me go, as she liked clubbing, but Maren didn't want her to go anywhere until she finished her work in the studio.

Maren set up a date for me with a male model named Stefano so I wouldn't show up alone. Going to a club without a date was something Kari would never do, even though she still sort of considered Michael her boyfriend. In her words, "We're taking a break, not breaking up."

On the appointed night, Kari left her entourage and came over to Maren's house to check out my hair, outfit, and glitterfication. Not only did I have sparkly body lotion and crystals in my manicure and pedicure, I had half a bottle of gold glitter sprinkled and then sprayed into place in my hair.

Kari had an arrangement with Lorenzo Rafael, one of the Hollywood elite fashion designers, to wear his outfits to openings, premieres, and award ceremonies. He even paid her two hundred thousand dollars a year for doing it. It was pure advertising for his label.

I thought this was an extremely sweet deal for her, until Maren handed me the dress I had to put on. Imagine a tan fake-leather top and matching miniskirt, with dark tan strips of fake leather hanging from the skirt—a pseudo Roman soldier look.

"You're kidding," I told Kari when she handed it to me.

Maren said, "Lorenzo Rafael likes to make a statement with his clothes."

"Yes," I said, "and that statement is: Bring out the gladiators."

Kari looked at me and sighed. "I don't know why you're complaining. I'm the one who's going to be trashed in the entertainment magazines for having no taste." Her gaze ran over the dress again. "I'll be snickered at by other celebrities and openly mocked on *Entertainment Tonight*. Fashion isn't a competition, you know. It's a blood sport."

"Can't you tell Lorenzo that you don't like this outfit?"

She shook her head. "I don't want to tick him off. He's making me a hand-sewn silk gown for the Grammys. It's going to have five pounds of beads on it."

Great. She got to wear silk, and I got to wear Xena: Warrior Princess.

After I dressed, Kari fussed over my hair and makeup,

giving me club etiquette tips. She slipped lip gloss, my cell phone, and mints into a small over-the-shoulder purse that Lorenzo had made to match my outfit. I would not only look like a gladiator, I would look like a gladiator with a purse. Kari handed it to me with a proud smile. "It's like you're my little sister and you're going to the prom."

I nearly dropped the purse. I couldn't look at her, afraid she would see the truth in my eyes. When I did return my gaze to her, she studied my features so intently my heart pounded against my chest. I waited for her to make the connection. Instead she dragged me in front of the bathroom mirror, and we stood side by side comparing our reflections.

"You look just like me—except for your nose." She turned to Maren, who stood in the doorway watching us. "I like Alexia's nose better than mine. What do you think? Should I get work done on mine?"

Maren said, "You need to finish your album before you do anything so drastic. How is the latest song going anyway? Did you get the feel you wanted?"

Kari walked out of the bathroom to the living room. She sank down into the love seat, somehow still managing to look ultrafeminine, even though she'd sprawled herself over the cushions. "I'm spending time relaxing so I can fill myself with creative energy before I start on it again."

Maren walked over until she stood directly in front of Kari. "Before you start again? You were supposed to be done with it by now."

"You can't rush your muse. They don't punch time clocks."

I glanced at my watch. Ten minutes after nine. My driver, a middle-aged guy named Bao-Zhi would be here soon with my bodyguard and Stefano. I wasn't sure what country Bao-Zhi came from. I'd only talked to him briefly before—briefly because he didn't speak much English. Mostly he just smiled, nodded, and checked his GPS. I think that was part of Maren's plan to keep my identity a secret. My staff was completely made up of foreigners. That way, there was less chance of them figuring out who I was, or leaking anything about me to the press. At any rate, it was almost time to leave. "Any last words of advice?" I asked.

Kari drew her gaze back to me. "Be careful when you're eating appetizers. If the paparazzi get pictures of you, the last thing I want to see is a photo of me with spinach quiche stuck between my teeth."

"Um, okay," I said.

Maren reviewed my appearance one last time. "I've given instructions to Stefano that he's to be attentive but not overly physical, so if you have any problems in that area, call my cell."

"Okay."

"Don't make out with Stefano," Kari said. "I don't want that in the tabloids, either."

"I don't even know the guy," I said.

She cocked her head as though she hadn't heard me.

"Although if he's really cute, you can snuggle with him. It won't hurt to have Michael get a *little* jealous."

Maren pulled a picture from a stack of paper on an end table and handed it to Kari. Kari let out a low whistle. "He *is* cute." She handed the picture back to Maren but looked over at me. "Okay, you can make out a little. That would totally bother Michael."

I walked over to Maren and reached for the picture. "I'm not making out with guys so your boyfriend will be jealous. That's not part of my job description."

I looked at the picture. The guy was stunning. "Well, maybe one kiss," I said.

The doorbell rang, and I shoved the picture back to Maren and turned toward the door.

"Have fun!" Kari called.

"Glide!" Maren reminded me.

I slowed down and made my walk smoother.

"One more thing," Maren said. "If you mess up and blow your cover—then you're a celebrity imposter who crashed the club. The real Kari is home sick, and we've never seen you before." And on that note of confidence, I left.

CHAPTER 7

Nikolay, my bodyguard, sat up in front of the limo, a look of dour seriousness never leaving his face. I knew he worked for me, but he just seemed like a really muscular version of a chaperone.

Stefano sat in the back of the limo with me, and he was just as beautiful as his photo. I wished I could use the camera on my cell phone to take my picture with him and send it to Lori—or better yet, send it to Theresa and Trevor. Who cared about the stupid Sadie Hawkins dance? I was in a limo with a specimen of a hundred percent male hunkiness.

Instead, I made small talk with Stefano as Bao-Zhi drove us to the club. Well, I tried to make small talk, anyway. Mostly Stefano talked about the shoots he'd done in Paris and Milan, dropped names of celebrities in the fashion world, and checked the time on his Rolex. I knew it was a Rolex because he pointed it out to me three times.

I wanted to tell him, "Okay, you've proved your point. You're rich and well connected. Please talk about something besides your stupid expensive watch." Instead, I nodded and smiled.

When the limo finally pulled up to the club, I saw a line of people waiting outside. Every single one of them turned and watched the car. A wave of anxiety swept over me, and

I instantly regretted the whole thing. I shouldn't have come to California. I should have been back home listening to Abuela complain about humidity, taxes, and how many commercials she had to sit through. I should have been sitting on Lori's couch watching stars on TV, not pretending to be one.

Nikolay got out of the limo first and opened the car door for us. Stefano followed, then held his hand out for me. As I emerged from the car, a thrilled gasp moved through the crowd. I heard Kari's name repeated over and over again. So many camera flashes went off around me that I felt like I was in the middle of a fireworks display. For a moment, I couldn't move at all. I'm not sure if it was nerves or just the surprise that so much attention, so much adoration was aimed in my direction. This is why I had prepared nonstop for weeks. I was a superstar.

Stefano pulled me forward. My anxiety dropped away, replaced by warm elation. Each flash was a kiss blown in my direction. I was beautiful, famous, and most important, loved. I gave the crowd one of Kari's over-the-shoulder grins, then let Stefano lead me into the club.

Once the three of us were inside, the owner, a man who didn't look much older than Stefano, hurried over and introduced himself. His hair was slicked back, he wore all black, and when I gave him my hand to shake, he took it to his lips and kissed it. I didn't know men did that and had no idea how to react. Did I laugh or pretend that hand kissing was normal? Maren hadn't covered this area. Fortunately, the owner didn't wait for a response. Still holding my hand between his, he said, "You're even more gorgeous in real life, Miss Kingsley. Anytime you want to hang somewhere, consider this your home away from home."

I thanked him and wondered how Kari ever got used to this sort of treatment. If I were her, I would go out every night just to see people's faces light up.

The owner showed us around the club. I had to pass up the good appetizers in favor of grapes and cheese since I was pretending to be a vegetarian. After that, Nikolay leaned up against a wall looking for suspicious activity while Stefano and I danced. Club dancing, I noticed right away, was nothing like dancing at my school dances. Some of the people looked more like they were trying to conceive children than actually dance, and I had to keep averting my gaze from them. If Abuela had been here, she would have wanted to smack people with her Bible left and right.

The club played a couple of Kari's songs, and when they did, a whole bunch of people sang along and turned to watch me. It was another aspect Maren hadn't covered, and I panicked at the awkwardness of the moment. I did some of the moves Jacqueline had taught me and pretended to sing along too.

We danced for two hours, and I noticed I was leaving trails of glitter all over the floor. I hoped the owner didn't mind. A few times, people came over to say that they loved my songs, but Stefano always whisked me away before they could attach themselves or try to become my new BFFs. Stefano got high marks for crowd control. He got lower marks for the way he'd taken to staring into my eyes intently, as though we were soul mates and not out on our first date.

Finally we left the dance floor to get drinks. Nikolay followed without getting too close, his eyes patrolling the crowd. I sipped a guava-kiwi juice while we walked toward the tables. A group of way-too-excited girls hurried by us without noticing me. "He's here?" one said with an exaggerated gasp. "Really?"

"I'm going to die!"

"I have to get a dance with him. I have to!"

I let my gaze follow them. To Stefano I said, "Who are they talking about?"

He pulled my chair out for me, then sat down himself. "Probably Grant Delray. He came in earlier."

"He did?" I asked, sounding too much like the girls we'd just passed. I calmed my voice and casually added, "I didn't know he was coming tonight."

"I saw him while we danced. Do you know him?"

Good question. I had no idea. Maren had never said anything about him, but that didn't mean Kari and he hadn't done something together. And he might know her well enough to spot a fake.

This could turn bad quickly.

Stefano laughed. "Judging from your response, I'd say you *do* know him." He leaned closer, and his voice took on a teasing edge. "You look uncomfortable, so it must be a good story."

"That's not it at all," I said. "I just suddenly remembered that . . ."

I had come to California to find out who I was, and I learned something about myself right then—I am not a good liar. I needed a reason to call Maren and talk to her privately, and my mind was a complete blank.

I rifled through my purse until I had my cell phone. "I, um, forgot to turn off my sprinklers and they're probably flooding the lawn by now. I need to call my assistant and tell her to turn them off."

His eyebrows drew together at this new piece of information. "You don't have landscapers to do that sort of thing?"

Which is why you shouldn't try to think up excuses for rich people.

I stood up. "Usually I do, but I thought the lawn was looking dry, so I turned the water on, and now I need to find a quiet place to make a call."

He frowned. "Why don't you text her?"

Because with the way Stefano kept draping himself around my shoulders, he was bound to see what I texted, and I couldn't very well write *Grant Delray is here. Does he know Kari?*

"My assistant might have questions."

Stefano stood up as though he would come with me, and I waved him to sit back down.

"You don't have to come. In fact I'll probably stop by the restroom too, so I'll be a few minutes."

Nikolay had seen me stand up and he walked over, ready

to shadow me, but I didn't want him as an audience either. "You don't need to come," I said. "Really, I'll be okay from here to the ladies' room."

I turned and walked away before he could reply. I'd find the owner and ask him if I could use his office. As I walked, I chided myself for being so easily rattled. One unforeseen thing happened and I'd gone off about sprinklers. I could have just used the restroom excuse in the first place. That would have given me enough time to make a phone call to Maren. If Kari knew Grant—if he could identify her—I'd fake a headache and make a night of it.

I hadn't gotten very far when I realized I'd made another mistake. Maren had warned me that I shouldn't go into crowds by myself. It was too easy to get swarmed. First a couple of guys asked if they could take my picture with their cell phone, then a girl wanted my autograph. In seconds, an entire crowd had surrounded me. People were actually shoving each other and jostling me. I said, "Look, I'm sorry. I need to get through," but no one listened. They waved pens in my direction and pushed their way next to me so that their friends could get pictures.

I felt bubbles of panic rising in my chest. Why hadn't I taken my bodyguard with me? Could he see this happening? Would my Warrior Princess dress stay put if someone pushed me over? I hoped so, since everyone here seemed to have a camera phone.

"Break it up!" a male voice yelled. "Come on, back off, unless you want the bouncer hauling you outside!"

At once, the crowd drained away, leaving me shaken but, thankfully, alone. I expected to see Nikolay. Instead Grant Delray, flanked by two towering men—probably his body-guards—stood in front of me.

I stared back at Grant in awe. I'd heard his songs on the radio hundreds of times. I had a few of them memorized, and now here he was in blue-eyed, bronzed-skin real life. And the picture of him on that magazine cover—it didn't do justice to his broad shoulders or pecs.

But another part of me was frozen in fear, waiting to see if he said, "Hey, you're not Kari Kingsley."

He raised an eyebrow. "Most people would say thanks at this point."

"Thanks," I said.

He rolled his eyes, clearly unimpressed with my grati-tude, then returned his gaze to my face, letting his eyes linger there longer than normal. He was studying me. I felt my face flush pink. Did he know the truth?

Nikolay walked up beside me. "You all right, Miss Kingsley?"

So he had seen the crowd descend on me, after all. I nod-ded, still afraid to speak while Grant was staring at me.

Grant motioned toward the dance floor without taking his eyes from me. "Let's dance—that's what we're getting paid for. Then I want to talk to you."

"Okay."

He took hold of my arm and I walked beside him, breathing deeply. I wanted to say something; I felt like I should, but somehow having three bodyguards trailing us made small talk impossible.

If Grant knew I was a fake, it didn't seem like he would expose me right now. But what did he want to talk about later? That didn't seem to be the kind of thing you said to someone you'd never met. I found it hard to think clearly about any of this, since my mind was mostly concentrating on the fact that Grant Delray was touching my arm.

We walked to a raised pedestal on the dance floor and as we did, the DJ changed the song that had been playing to one of Grant's. People noticed us and sang along. Grant danced—and not your average guy dancing, he danced as though performing on stage. He was all muscle and rhythm, movement and glide. I watched him so intently I nearly forgot to dance myself. I tried; my feet kept moving to the beat, but I looked pitiful next to him. Which meant maybe Jacqueline had a point after all and I should listen to her better.

Grant didn't look at me while he danced. But every once in a while, his gaze would connect with mine and then I'd quickly glance away so he wouldn't see me staring. Kari wouldn't gape at him like some groupie. Even if he did have deep blue eyes, a square jaw, and touchable brown hair with golden highlights.

People snapped pictures of us with their cell phones, and even though it was too dark on the dance floor for them to turn out, I really wished I could ask someone to forward a picture to me. Whether he knew I was a fake or not, I *so* wanted a souvenir of this moment.

The dance finally ended, and the people around us clapped. Grant took hold of my arm with one hand and waved at the crowd with the other, then led me off the platform.

To tell you the truth, I'd completely forgotten about Stefano until I saw him glaring at us from the corner of the dance floor. He walked up to me and thrust his hand in the air between us. "You left your sprinklers running, eh? The next time you want to get rid of a guy, tell him the truth." Then he turned around and stalked away.

Grant raised his eyebrows. "Is that where you were going—to turn your sprinklers off? When did you start doing your own yard work?"

I didn't answer, just looked at Stefano's back retreating into the crowd. I should go after him. Only I couldn't. Not when Grant Delray wanted to talk to me. I had to find out what he wanted, didn't I?

"So you really were ditching him?" Grant asked.

I didn't know how to answer. Saying "No, I wanted to be with you instead" sounded borderline starstruck, which Kari wouldn't be, even if I was.

When I didn't go after Stefano, Grant laughed under his breath, then took hold of my hand again and pulled me toward the back of the club.

"You could have least told him 'I left something on the stove.' That's nearly believable."

He spoke to me so casually, like he knew Kari. Maybe he hadn't realized I was a fake in the low lighting of the club, but we were heading toward a back door with a sign that read EMPLOYEES ONLY. Would his tone of voice change then? A bouncer stood by the wall, surveying the crowd. When he saw us and our entourage of bodyguards he said, "Is there anything I can get for you, Mr. Delray, Miss Kingsley?"

"We need a place to talk alone for a few minutes."

The bouncer stepped aside—just like that—and let us by. Grant opened the door and we walked into a supply room, leaving the bodyguards outside. He hit the light switch and I blinked, adjusting my eyes to the harsh white glare. I was afraid to turn and face him, so I stared at boxes stacked against the wall labeled NAPKINS, CUPS, STRAWS.

"I don't know why I'm telling you this," Grant said tightly. "I shouldn't feel obligated after what you've done."

He knew then. He knew I was a fake. I turned to him, trying to think of the right words to plead my case. I had considered the fact that I might not be able to pull this charade off. I had even thought out justifications for my position when I got caught, but I had never once thought I'd be busted by Grant Delray in a supply closet.

Before I could say anything, he went on. "I guess I'm telling you this because, despite everything, I hate it when people make a profit trashing celebrities, and this time I feel partially responsible. So I'm giving you fair warning. You know I helped Lorna Beck get a job?"

"What?" I asked.

"Lorna Beck. I got her a job working for my agent. She's his personal assistant now."

"Oh." Maybe he didn't know who I was. That was good news, except that I had no idea what he was talking about.

"She's a good assistant—has a photographic memory. You might not have realized that about her."

I smiled. It seemed like I should. After all, he got someone a job, and she was good at it. "That's great," I said.

His eyebrows drew together at my words, and he scanned my face to see if I was serious. "You think that's great?"

Which meant I'd given the wrong reaction, but I didn't know why. I swallowed hard. "I mean, I'm glad your agent likes Lorna. . . ." That seemed like a safe statement.

More doubt shadowed his face. He took a step closer, examining my expression. "You're serious." This seemed to surprise him. "You don't hold any bad feelings for her?"

I shrugged. "Why should I?" And I wasn't being rhetorical. I really wanted to know.

"Well, you're the one who fired her. Remember that entire bit about 'you'll never work in this business again'?"

Oh. Kari had fired Lorna. That was an important detail, but how was I supposed to react now?

Right there staring at the paper towel box, I decided that as long as I was being Kari, she could be gracious about her ex-employees. I nodded sadly. "Right, well, sometimes in the heat of the moment, we all say things we don't mean, and I'm sorry about that. Really. I'm happy she's got a good job now."

"Uh-huh." He watched me, still not convinced.

"Tell her I said hi the next time you see her."

He folded his arms and regarded me silently.

It was easy to smile back at him because I was Kari and she was important enough to hold his attention. For the first time since I'd become her, I really relished her status. I was looking at Grant Delray, and he was staring back at me with deep blue eyes. "Is that all you wanted to talk about?"

He shook his head. "No. I thought you should know she's writing a tell-all book about you."

"What?" I took a step backward. "What is she saying about me?"

"That you're a gambling addict, for one thing."

"I am not." The denial came out before I could fully process that he meant Kari. I had no idea if she was or not.

"Lorna says you owe half a million dollars to casinos, and she's seen the documentation herself—dates, amounts. She's got photographic recall." He said this as a challenge. He expected me to deny it or explain it away. I couldn't do either.

"She's an ex-employee with an ax to grind," I said, perhaps more to myself than to Grant. I didn't want the claim to be true, even if it did make sense, and maybe it did. Kari had brought me in to make money. Why would she take the risk unless she needed the money fast? I hated the thought of being used that way—to pay off casinos.

I didn't want to hear any more bad things about Kari—my sister—and yet I had to ask. "What else is Lorna saying?"

Grant didn't speak for a moment, his expression turned from accusing to something else, contemplative maybe. His voice had gone quiet. "That you're a spoiled prima donna, raised with a silver microphone in your mouth. I don't know a lot, only the things my agent has let slip—"

"Is she saying anything about my father?"

My question seemed to take him aback. "What are you afraid she'll say?"

I was afraid if anyone dug into Kari's past—or her father's past—they would turn up information about my mother and me. The thought of my life being laid open that way made my throat feel tight. Would the tabloids try to track my mother down? Would they come after me?

"I don't know," I said. "I just want her to leave my family out of it. If she has something against me, that's one thing. I might deserve it, but they don't." I realized my mistake after I'd spoken. I had referred to my family as "they" instead of "he." Kari only had her father as her family.

Grant's eyebrows rose, but if he noticed my mistake, he didn't mention it. "I don't know what she's saying about your father."

"Can you find out what's in the book?"

"You mean like ask to see the table of contents or something?"

"Wouldn't Lorna tell you?"

He put his hand on his chest in disbelief. "You're asking me for a favor? Me?"

I weighed his words and then decided I should answer him anyway. "Yes."

He tilted his head, blinking. "And what did you say when I asked you for a favor?"

Well, that was a question I couldn't answer. Although I imagined it was some sort of no since he was acting like I'd sprouted a second head. I shrugged and held my hands out to him as though reaching to make amends—anything rather than stand there and stare at him like I had no idea what he meant.

"You said you didn't do appearances unless you got paid," he said. "And your fee for singing was twenty thousand dollars." He walked to the door, resting one hand on the doorknob. "How about this—I'll do a book review for you for the same price."

Then he walked out and left me standing there among the boxes.

CHAPTER 8

I stayed there longer than I should have. I bet real celebrities don't hide out in supply closets full of boxes of straws, but I needed time to process everything Grant had said. When I came out, I asked Nikolay to escort me to the limo.

Instead of going back to Maren's house like I was supposed to, I told the driver to take me to my house—Kari's house. I needed to talk to her.

The gate code wasn't a problem. That had been easy enough to remember from when we dropped her off from the airport: It was 1111. I think as in "I'm number one" repeated four times.

There was one awkward moment while Nikolay escorted me to the door. I worried that it would be locked and then I'd have to make up some excuse about losing my keys, which would cause Nikolay to walk around the house checking for open windows. My mind was already racing ahead to the moment that Kari called the police to report burglars, and the scene down at the police station when the police—and then the media—realized I'd been at a club opening impersonating Kari Kingsley.

How would my mug shot look in this gladiator dress?

But the door swung open. I didn't want Kari to freak out if she unexpectedly heard her front door opening, so as I walked in I called out, "Hey, I'm back from the club!" Which—in case Nikolay heard me—is something Kari might have said, if she was one of those people who talked to her cats.

I shut the door firmly, then leaned against it, waiting for Kari to appear. While I waited I took in the entryway. In my house, you walked into the living room and from there you could see the kitchen and the hallway that led to the three small bedrooms that made up the rest of the house. Kari had an entryway the size of my living room, but you couldn't see anything beyond it. All you saw was this wall with a huge black-and-white picture of Kari wearing a cowboy hat and sitting in a wheat field. It even had its own lights aimed at it.

Stone tiles spread out in front of me, and on either side of the entryway were matching antique chests. A lamp and a silk plant sat on one. The other had a decorative bowl full of funky black and white balls.

After a minute, Kari appeared. She wore an oversized football shirt that must have doubled as pajamas and carried a corn dog. She cocked her head when she saw me. "What are you doing here?"

I pointed at her corn dog. "What are you doing with that? I thought you were a vegetarian."

She looked down at the food in her hand. "Oh, this. Sometimes when I'm stressed-out I have to have comfort food. Besides, this hardly counts as meat. It's all preservatives and nitrates."

I took a step toward her, still pointing. "I had to pass up coconut shrimp appetizers at the club and you're here eating a corn dog?"

"Save the lecture and tell me how things went." She gave me a teasing smile. "Especially things with Stefano. Did you kiss him?"

I folded my arms. "Stefano left the club after I danced with another guy."

Kari took a bite of her corn dog and shook her head. "Well, good riddance, then. I totally hate jealous guys. That was the problem with Michael; he got too demanding, you know? I mean, my boyfriend has to realize that I'm going to smile and flirt with a lot of people. That's just the business. A guy should deal with it, not retaliate by partying with some trampy little starlet from *General Hospital*."

"I was dancing with Grant Delray. Do you want to fill me in on why he hates you?"

"Grant Delray?" She put her corn dog down on the antique chest with a thud. "He was there?"

"Yeah. We had an interesting talk. Mostly interesting because I didn't know what he was talking about—"

Kari cut me off. "He was not supposed to be there. I have made it clear to anyone I deal with that I am never going to be in the same place as that egotistical, hypocritical, kiss-up publicity hog. I'm calling Maren about this right now. This is absolutely—"

"He said someone named Lorna Beck is writing a tell-all book about you."

Kari didn't speak. She let out a shrill "Nooooo!" picked up a lamp, and threw it against the wall. It smashed and little chunks skittered across the tile, spinning to a stop.

How much had that cost? At least two hundred dollars. I couldn't help myself; I thought of things that two hundred dollars could buy. A year's worth of cold cereal? Six months of cell phone coverage? A dozen T-shirts? One broken lamp.

Kari ran her hand through her hair and took deep, labored breaths. "She can't do this. She signed a nondisclosure contract. I will sue her. I will sue her publisher, and I will sue any store that carries her book!"

This is what Grant had expected to see, I realized. He'd thought I would fall apart like Kari was doing now. Maybe she would have thrown those boxes of straws against the wall and then they would have rained down like confetti on the two of them. I was glad I had been there instead.

"So the stuff about the gambling debts is true?"

Kari put her hand over her mouth, sank onto the floor crying, and didn't answer me.

I called Maren. I didn't know what else to do. Then I sat next to Kari on the entryway floor. I hated to see her this way, so fragile and hurt, her flair and confidence gone. A real sister would know what to do in this sort of situation, but I had nothing to draw on.

I scooted over until we were almost touching, then I patted her arm awkwardly. "It will be all right. Things can't be that bad."

Kari held one hand over her eyes. "Lorna will make things look that bad—and Grant will probably give away copies of her book at his concerts."

I thought of Grant, of him taking my arm and leading me to the floor, and how my heart had flipped around in my chest so persistently it had been hard to dance at all. I remembered his blue eyes, cool with resentment, staring at me in the supply room, and his expression when he'd left. I wanted to hate him for Kari's sake, but perhaps his blue eyes were still too vibrant in my memory. I could only muster some disappointment that he would never like me. "How come you don't get along with Grant? And why did he act like he knew you but didn't recognize I wasn't you?"

"I've never actually met him," she said, her voice uneven from crying. "We've only talked through our publicists. A few months ago, Grant put together a fund-raiser for the Sun Ridge Children's Hospital, and he wanted me to appear as one of the headliners. And since it was a fund-raiser he wanted it for free."

Kari took a shuddering breath. "I refused. I get requests to do fund-raisers all the time—and I mean every single day. My policy is that I do two free ones a year, and that's it. I've already done one for California animal shelters and one for breast cancer, and besides, right now I really need money. I've even had to let a lot of my staff go. If I'm going to take off work to practice and put on a concert, I need to be paid. I've got to buy a costume, have a choreographer come up with something new, pay the backup dancers, the makeup artist, the hairstylist—my glam squad is expensive. I gave him a cut-rate price for a mini concert."

That was why Grant didn't like her? Because she hadn't done his fund-raiser for free? Inwardly my opinion of Grant slid downward. What was it with these celebrities that they always had to get what they wanted?

"I thought the whole thing had ended," Kari said, "but then a few weeks later, Lorna—she was still my assistant then—Lorna gave out my cell phone number to the hospital director so he could call and lay a guilt trip on me about how the sick kids really wanted to see me and couldn't I just come make an appearance and sing a couple of songs?

"I couldn't believe Lorna had given out my number. It was so completely unprofessional, and I'd already said no. She put me in a bad situation, making me turn them down all over again. And I had to change my phone number too. Once those things get out to the public, they always go viral. Of course I fired her.

"So Grant—Mr. Higher and Mightier Than Anyone Else, since he obviously cares about sick kids more than I do—he got her a new job. A job where apparently she has enough free time to write an entire book trashing me." Her voice broke again. "That's going to kill my endorsements—I've been talking to some department stores about doing a clothing line . . . and my agent is working on a movie deal with Disney, and Mattel wants to do Kari Kingsley doll because I'm such a good role model. Now my fans will turn on me." She didn't say more. She went back to crying.

"Don't worry about the book." I patted her arm again, this time less awkwardly. "It's not like most people read anymore. Well, not unless the book has a wizard school or a hot vampire. And as a Kari Kingsley expert, I'm absolutely certain your life has neither of those things."

She let out a halfhearted laugh, then put her head on her knees. "The paparazzi will gather in packs to hunt me down."

"You could always dye your hair brown and hang out with my family in West Virginia. The paparazzi would never find you there. We could do the prince and the pauper."

"What's the prince and the pauper?"

"See?" I said. "You just proved my point. No one reads anymore."

She lifted her head. "Oh, you mean that book by Mark Twain. I remember it now. As my life went flashing before my eyes, I recognized it in my eighth-grade English class."

"Your life only flashes before your eyes when you're dying," I said.

"Or when you find out someone is writing a tell-all book about you—at least the really bad parts flash before your eyes." She let out a moan and rested her head in her hands.

I put my arm around her, giving her a side hug. This moment more than any other made her feel like my sister, only I felt like the older sister instead of the younger one.

Maren came not long after that. She took a look at the broken lamp, then helped Kari to her feet and put her arm around her shoulders. Her voice, which had always been so brisk and businesslike with me, dripped with consolation. "It's okay. I'll talk to your lawyer, and we'll take care of this." She patted Kari's arm soothingly. "You shouldn't have to deal with people like Lorna and Grant. You leave everything to me."

To me she said, "I've called your driver. He'll take you to my house." Then the two of them walked out of the entryway, leaving me there. That's when the full weight of Kari's words hit me. If the press got wind of Lorna's book and gathered in packs to hunt her down, I could very well be the one they found.

· · ·

When Maren came back to the town house several hours later, I was sitting in the kitchen looking up information on gambling addiction with my laptop. She glanced at the screen, tossed her keys on the table, and sighed.

"Does Kari have a gambling addiction?" I asked.

"No, you don't have an addiction, just a love of playing cards and an unfortunate losing streak. You're taking responsibility for your debts, though, and paying them off."

I flipped from one screen to another. "I'm not asking for the official position, I'm asking if Kari has a problem."

"All you need to know is the official position."

I held my hand out to the computer screen, offering it as proof. "This is serious. Kari needs help. She needs counseling."

Maren laughed and turned away from me, walking to the cupboards to pull out a glass. As she poured herself a drink, she said, "See, this is the problem with Lorna's allegations. You tell a normal person that Kari Kingsley owes four hundred and eighty thousand dollars to casinos, the only assumption they can make is that she's a gambling addict. People don't realize that it's not unusual for wealthy people to blow five, ten thousand dollars on a night of entertainment."

"Even if they've already lost hundreds of thousands of dollars?"

Maren leaned against the counter, the red lipstick she wore still as vibrant as it had been in the morning. "I know celebrities who spend that much going to Cannes every year. And to tell you the truth, Kari owes more than that on her credit cards. Her favorite way to waste time is shopping." Maren slowly swirled the contents of her drink. "But now that I'm her manager, we're changing that. I have her on a strict budget, she's selling off the Lamborghini she hardly ever drives, and no more clothes shopping or gambling until her debts are paid." She took a drink, set her glass on the countertop, and ran her fingers through her hair. "Kari's real problem is that she's dragging her feet on her next album. She records a song and then decides she doesn't like it. But when the new album comes out, she won't have any problem paying off the rest of her debts. Until then, you'll do appearances so she can focus on singing. As long as she can make payments on her debts, the casinos will keep quiet about what she owes."

Maren walked toward her bedroom, kicking her shoes off, but then she bent down to pick them up. She never left her shoes lying around.

"What about Lorna?" I called after her. "Is there a way to stop her?"

"I'll look into that tomorrow," she said. "Lorna did sign a nondisclosure contract, so we'd win in court. But the problem is that sometimes when you threaten to sue a publisher, they see it as free advertising. It's like adding fuel to the fire. Nothing sells print quite as well as a scandal." She turned around and surveyed me for another moment. When she spoke again, her voice was impatient. "But you don't need to worry about Kari or pry into her life. Your job is to be her when you're needed. That's all. And don't go over to Kari's house again unless I okay it. If you find out anything else you think she needs to know, you tell me first. Understood?"

I felt the sting of her reprimand. "All right."

But after she left, I kept reading about gambling addiction. The prognosis for people who didn't get help seemed bleak. They faced financial ruin, estrangement from their families, thoughts of hopelessness and despair. A lot of them ended up in jail or committed suicide.

Then again, maybe Maren was right and I was worrying about nothing. Maybe four hundred eighty thousand wasn't a big deal to people who spent eight hundred dollars for a pair of shoes and broke lamps when they were angry.

The image of the glass shards on the floor stayed in my mind, bothering me. Maybe because it reminded me of the way I'd pushed books onto the floor in the library, the way I'd stormed out on my mother. Perhaps besides our mannerisms, our love of horses, and weaknesses for Almond Joys, we also shared a temper.

Seeing it in Kari made me realize for the first time that I didn't like it in myself.

I did an Internet search on Sun Ridge Children's Hospital. They'd already had the fund-raising concert. Dozens of pictures from the event dotted their website. I found myself staring extra long at the ones of Grant. They didn't do him justice. They couldn't capture the energy of his movements or the way his gaze sliced through you. Next I noticed the pictures of the children. There was a girl who couldn't have been more than ten—completely bald, but still smiling. I wondered if I would be able to smile like that after chemotherapy. I looked from face to face, my heart squeezing tighter with each set of eyes I looked into.

How could Kari have turned them down?

How could she get requests like this every day and not go crazy with grief?

I finally turned off the computer and went to bed, but the faces stayed in my mind long after I'd shut my eyes.

• • •

I woke up early the next morning thanks to a phone call from Abuela. She either didn't get the whole concept of the three-hour time difference or she didn't care.

"Were you still sleeping?" she asked after I gurgled out a hello. "It's nearly lunchtime."

"Which is eight o'clock California time." This was the one day Maren had let me sleep in because I'd been out late, and it figured that Abuela would call.

"I'll tell you what time it is. It's time you came home." She lowered her voice. "*Escúchame.*" Listen to me. "Your mother went out with Larry again last night. You need to know that."

I lay back down on my bed and let my cell phone rest against my face. "Why do I need to know that?"

"Because that's two times in one week," she said. "He had her over to his house last Wednesday to watch TV."

TV. He really knew how to woo a girl.

"What am I supposed to do about that?" I asked.

Abuela's voice took on a terse tone. "The only reason your mother is getting serious with him is because she thinks you need a father figure. You're so starved for one that you ran off to California, and heaven knows what other fool-minded things you'll do in an effort to have someone who was never worth it to begin with take notice of you."

"What?" I asked suddenly, shaking off the remnants of sleep. "Did my mom say that to you?"

"Your mother and I discuss you. It's not gossip, since we love you. Your mother thinks that man is going to break your heart the same way he broke hers, and she wants a healthy example of male nurturing in your life for when you wise up and come on back home. If you came home now, we could all save ourselves grief. You won't have to meet Alex Kingsley, and I won't have to see my daughter marry a man who can speak nonstop through dinner about tax law."

"Okay. I'll talk to her about it."

"I don't have many more years left on this earth, Lexi. Don't make me spend them with Larry."

"I said I'd talk to her."

"You're going to college in a few months, so what do you need a male role model for anyway?"

"Okay, Abuela, I've got to go now. Good-bye." I hung up the phone and stared at the ceiling for a while.

I didn't think my mother would really marry Larry just to provide me with a father, but that didn't mean she wouldn't marry him for other reasons. Maybe if your teenage daughter is meeting her rich, famous father for the first time, you want to feel like you have a stable, successful man in your life.

I dragged myself out of bed and went to the kitchen for breakfast. There was no point in calling Mom now. She was at work.

Maren had gone. She'd left a cut grapefruit sitting on the table and a note saying she went to meet with Kari's lawyer. I ignored the grapefruit and made myself toast. She also left me instructions to practice my dancing routines, but since it was Saturday and Jacqueline wouldn't even be at the dance studio, I ignored that too. I had other plans for the morning.

I went to Maren's office. Last week when I'd been autographing pictures of Kari to send out to fans, I'd noticed a boxful of Kari's last CD. I took about thirty of them and shoved them into a tote bag.

Then I called my driver and asked him to pick me up in forty-five minutes. Maren never said I couldn't leave the house. She'd just said I couldn't go to Kari's house. I showered, trying to remove all the lingering glitter from my hair, then dressed and re-created my hair and makeup the way I'd been taught—shading my nose to make it seem sharper, applying thick eyeliner and dramatic eye shadow.

I'd just finished when Bao-Zhi came. It occurred to me during the ride down to the hospital that I should call Kari to make sure she wasn't out somewhere doing a public appearance while I showed up elsewhere, but I didn't call her. I knew she'd been up late the night before, so she was most likely still asleep. Besides, she wouldn't want me to visit the hospital, not when it had been the heart of her most recent problem. This was one of those times it was better to ask forgiveness than permission.

I had Bao-Zhi escort me into the hospital lobby. He wasn't much of a bodyguard, but I didn't dare ask Nikolay. Real bodyguards like to ask a lot of security questions and tend to frown upon just randomly showing up places. If I had called him, I knew he'd tell Maren what I was doing.

The receptionist eyed me cautiously, but when I asked, she picked up her phone and put in a call to the director.

Not long afterward, he walked down the hallway. He was a tall man with a full head of hair and a politician's smile. He looked me over from head to foot with surprise. That was one of the oddest things about being Kari, how often and blatantly people stared at me. I no longer blended into the crowd. Without checking, I could tell I'd caught the attention of the entire lobby.

He held out his hand and shook mine with a firm grasp. "So glad to meet you, Miss Kingsley. What brings you here?"

"I felt bad I couldn't do your fund-raiser, and I wondered if I could meet some of the children."

His jaw dropped slightly, but after his shock wore off, he agreed to take me around. I met about twenty-five kids that morning. A boy in for hip surgery for his cerebral palsy. A girl getting skin grafts for third-degree burns. Way too many kids who were doing rounds of chemotherapy.

I sat on the bed and talked to some. I walked with one boy while his nurse pushed him around the grounds. Each time I came into a room, someone's face lit up with excitement. A mother visiting her daughter actually cried when she saw me. "Our whole family loves you," she said. "God bless you for coming."

Guilt and happiness both flooded through me at these times. People wouldn't have been so grateful if they'd known I was an imposter, but wasn't it worth it to make them happy? Weren't they better off that I'd come than if they kept thinking that Kari Kingsley was some unreachable celebrity who didn't care?

Each child seemed so brave. My problems—the worrying I'd done about money, about not being popular enough in high school, and about my father—all of them shrank in significance.

While I sat in the last room talking to a girl named Morgan and feeling that I really should have eaten more than toast before I left, I heard a noise and looked up.

Grant Delray stood in the doorway.

CHAPTER 9

I couldn't read Grant's expression. It wasn't surprise, approval, or disapproval. He just watched me. Morgan looked over and gasped. "You're Grant Delray."

His gaze turned to her, and he smiled. "You caught me."

"I didn't know you were here too," she chimed. "Can I have your autograph?"

He strolled over to the bed and took the pen from my hand. "Sure thing. Where did you want me to sign?"

She grabbed the CD I'd given her. "Here—can you sign next to Kari's signature?"

As he wrote, he spoke out loud, "To Morgan, hope your surgery goes well. Remember when listening to this CD that you actually like me much better than Kari Kingsley."

I smacked him.

Morgan's gaze flicked to me, then back to him. "Kari is an amazing singer," she said.

My stomach rumbled loudly, and as Grant handed the CD back to her, he said, "It's true. Even Kari's stomach sings."

"Yes, and it hits the low notes much better than I do," I said. "But right now it's saying it's past time for lunch, so I'd better go."

I gave Morgan a hug good-bye, then stood up and left the

room. Grant came with me. We walked down the hallway together, neither of us moving very fast. Bao-Zhi walked even slower, following us far enough away that Grant and I had some privacy. I stole a glance at Grant's perfect profile. His hair wasn't mussed and gelled like it had been last night. It lay against his face in smooth brown waves. He wore jeans and a T-shirt, making him look like a normal guy. Well, assuming that the normal guy was really hot.

"It was nice of you to drop by and talk with the kids," he said.

"How did you know I was here?"

"My father called and told me. He's the director."

My head swung around to look at Grant. "He is?"

Grant smiled at my surprise, and I wondered if Kari already knew this information, in which case I'd made myself look really stupid.

"Neither one of us advertises it," he said. "My family likes to be left out of the limelight. My dad especially doesn't want to be inundated at work by girls asking for my phone number." He motioned with his head toward the lobby. "Although he does threaten to auction my number on eBay every time he needs a fund-raiser. That's why I'm always available."

"Well, he seems very nice."

Grant laughed, and I looked at him wondering what I'd said wrong.

He shook his head. "I just never imagined you'd be so polite."

I mentally chided myself. He was right. I'd never acted like Kari around him, but it seemed a little late for that now. Besides, being polite was good.

He said, "I guess since you put in an appearance here, I owe you a report on Lorna's book."

"That's not why I came."

He raised an eyebrow. "So you're saying you don't want a report?"

He had me there. "No, I want it."

"I'll see how much information I can get from my agent. Lorna gave him a copy because she wants his advice on how to get around her nondisclosure contract. That's how I found out about it."

"Isn't the whole point of a nondisclosure contract that she can't write a book?" I asked. I'd signed one myself, and it was pretty specific about that point.

His eyes shifted from the hallway to me. "She's claiming that you broke the contract by firing her without just cause, and she's betting that you don't want the conditions of her being fired brought out in court. Even if you stop her, your image is going to take some damage."

"That's so vindictive and malicious." The words came out of my mouth with too much surprise. Kari had been upset last night, but not surprised. Plus, Kari probably wouldn't have used the words *vindictive* and *malicious*. I made a mental note not to say any words I'd seen on the SAT vocabulary test.

"That's why I told you about it in the first place," Grant

said. "It's bad enough that so many people make money off celebrities. They shouldn't make money by stabbing us in the back. I wouldn't have helped her if I'd known she was going to do this."

"You were smart to help her," I said. "Now her sequel won't be *And Grant Delray Is a Jerk Too.*"

He laughed, and the two of us slowed our pace even further. We'd reached the lobby. He said, "Can I buy you some lunch, or are you one of those girls who lives on a diet of cucumbers and unbuttered popcorn?"

"Do you really want me to say, or would you rather read about it in Lorna's book?"

He tilted his head and smiled. "Actually, that's one of the things I already know about you from Lorna. You claim to be a vegetarian but you cheat."

"You know that?" I couldn't keep the happiness out of my voice. "Good—I am so craving a cheeseburger. With bacon."

He laughed at me again. "Okay, it's a date." He glanced back at Bao-Zhi and must have judged his bodyguard skills to be lacking. "There's a crowd forming in the parking lot outside the hospital. My dad can have the hospital security guard help you to your car, or you can ride with me. I'm parked in the back by the food service entrance."

I tried to make it sound like I actually considered the options before I said, "I'll ride with you." I turned back to Bao-Zhi. "Can you please bring the car to the front of the hospital like you're waiting for me to come out? That should keep the fans there until I leave."

Which was not only good crowd control, it meant I got to be alone with Grant.

I stepped closer to Bao-Zhi and whispered, "Don't tell Maren about this and you'll receive a really big tip."

A few minutes later, Grant and I climbed into his dark green Jaguar and drove to an ocean-side restaurant with private rooms. Our room had a great view of the beach, but I hardly looked at it. Sand and waves just didn't have the same appeal as sky blue eyes. Even though I really wanted a cheeseburger, I ordered an artichoke pasta salad because I was paranoid the waiter would tell the tabloids that I'd eaten meat. Grant changed his order to a bacon cheeseburger so we could switch meals after the waiter left. Really, he was such a nice guy.

Despite this fact, and the aforementioned hotness factor, I did not throw myself at him over lunch. I didn't even use *Seventeen* magazine's flirting tips with him. If pressed, I might admit that I smiled a lot, and maybe I had a hard time taking my eyes off of him, but I didn't flirt. It was pointless.

I couldn't tell him who I really was, and if he started liking me, then he might show up someplace the real Kari was. That would be a really bad end to my high-paying job, not to mention the end to the best chance I had to meet my father. Besides, Grant knew someone who was writing a book on Kari, and despite the fact that he was laughing and joking now, he would probably not think it was okay that I'd lied to a hospital full of sick kids, or that Kari paid me to deceive people. I did not want Lorna writing a chapter entitled "Alexia, the Illegitimate Sister, and Kari Kingsley, Imposter."

During a lull in the conversation he looked over, his eyes openly appraising, and said, "I can't get over how nice you are. Tell me again why you turned down the fund-raiser for the hospital?"

I was glad Kari had told me the answer to this question. "Well, you know I'm short on money right now. I couldn't afford the new outfit, the choreographer, the backup dancers—my glam squad is expensive."

"You could have showed up in jeans and a T-shirt and no one would have cared." He held a hand out as though offering the proof. "You didn't pay a makeup artist and a hairstylist to fix you up this morning, did you? You're beautiful the way you are."

I would have answered him, and I'm sure I would have said something really coherent too, except that I was too busy blushing and grinning like an idiot.

And then the waiter came to refill our water glasses and ask us if everything was okay.

Oh, yes. Things were so much better than okay. The coolest guy in existence had just said I was beautiful.

Lunch went by too fast and then Grant paid the bill and asked where I wanted him to drop me off. I told him I needed to go to my assistant's house. As we walked through the restaurant, every person we passed stopped and stared at us. For a few moments, I felt like I really was a celebrity walking beside Grant Delray. And I wasn't just walking, I was gliding. The walk was all about attitude, I realized; you couldn't help but glide when you felt this way.

As soon as we stepped out of the restaurant, I saw the paparazzi. Two men with huge cameras stood outside the door, along with a dozen people who were loitering around. How had they found us?

Stupid question. So many people had seen us walk in together. Any of them could have called someone. Why hadn't I considered this before I agreed to go to lunch?

Kari had given me strict instructions to either smile at or ignore anyone with a camera. "Don't scowl," Kari said. "Magazines love to use scowling pictures when they run horrible headlines about you."

So I smiled and told myself I was not allowed to rip the cameras out of their hands and clang them together like cymbals. While the shutters went off, one man asked, "Are the two of you dating?"

Yes, well, that would make an interesting story, wouldn't it? Maren was going to kill me. Kari was going to kill me even worse.

Grant shook his head like it was a foolish question. "Nope. We're just talking about doing a duet and donating the proceeds to Sun Ridge Children's Hospital. That's spelled: *S-U-N R-I-D-G-E*. It's going to be great, and we really appreciate your support in getting the word out to our fans."

Grant took hold of my arm then, probably because I stood frozen to the spot, hands gripped at my side. He towed me the rest of the way across the parking lot to his Jaguar.

Once we were both sitting inside and I'd stopped hyperventilating enough to speak, I said, "We're doing a duet? Where did that come from?"

He turned on the ignition and pulled out of the parking space. "You obviously still have a lot to learn about the paparazzi. The best chance you have of getting reporters not to use your story is if you tell them you want them to run it. They don't care about helping you advertise your latest cause. Everybody has one of those. They want something scandalous." He looked back over his shoulder to where the photographers were climbing in their cars. "My manager let all the news outlets know about the Sun Ridge fundraiser, and a total of one newspaper put a three-inch picture and write-up in the entertainment section. That was it."

"Oh," I said, and felt a little more relieved. Maybe those pictures wouldn't show up anywhere.

Grant eased the car out of the parking lot and onto the street. "Of course that doesn't mean we shouldn't do a duet. Actually, that's a brilliant idea." He took his eyes off the road to look at me. "You want to help those kids, and this time it wouldn't cost you anything but a little time. We could use my band. What do you think?"

I thought I had made a really big tactical mistake. I couldn't sing a duet with him. My singing voice sounded nothing like Kari's. She could hit notes I couldn't even swat at. "I'm already behind schedule on my next album," I said.

He turned his attention back to the road. "It doesn't have to be soon, just sometime. Think about it. Keep your eyes open for songs that would work, and I'll do the same, okay?"

What could I say to that? I couldn't think of a way to turn him down without sounding like I was hiding something.

"I'll talk to my manager about it," I said.

He said other things on the way to Maren's, but I hardly heard them. My mind was still stuck on the whole duet business. How in the world was I going to mention all of that plus the paparazzi pictures to Maren and Kari? Would they fire me right off? That's what Kari had done when Lorna had put her in an awkward situation. Was there any way I could keep it from them until May 13, when I met my father? It was still almost a month and a half away.

When we pulled up to Maren's town house, I was still running these sorts of mental calculations. Grant put the car in park but didn't turn it off. "Can I ask you a question?"

I grasped the door handle. "Sure."

"Are you still an item with Michael Jung?"

"No," I said, then I realized what he was really asking—he was about to ask me out, and I couldn't say yes, even though I would have loved to see him again. It was too dangerous. "I mean, we're taking a break, but we're still together."

"You're taking a break?" he asked.

"Yes."

"So are you allowed to see other people during your break?"

"Um, no." As soon as I said this I remembered Grant had seen me last night with Stefano. "Except professionally, like last night."

He nodded. "Can I have your phone number, then? Just for professional use. I'll need to contact you when I find more out about Lorna's book."

He smiled at me, and despite the fact that I couldn't encourage him, chills ran up my spine. Grant Delray wanted my phone number. I gave him my cell number, stepped out of his car, and then did a Kari Kingsley glide up the stairs to Maren's house.

I opened the door and found Maren in the living room waiting for me. Her arms were crossed, and her nostrils flared like a wild bull.

She stepped toward me, pinching her lips together. "The director of the Sun Ridge Children's Hospital just called to pass along their thanks. The patients were thrilled by your visit."

"They're sick little kids—" I started, but she didn't let me finish.

"It was a stupid thing to do!" she yelled, leaning until she was about six inches away from my face. Then she let out a stream of swearwords that would have put boys hanging out in a locker room to shame.

"You don't go out in public, and you don't pretend to be

Kari unless I okay it. You can't use her identity every time you think it would be fun to play celebrity. One mistake and you'll blow everything we've worked for. Do you understand? Do you?"

I nodded.

She took a step back, suddenly calm again. "If you play this right, you'll go home with a nice chunk of money. If you mess up, I'll deny I've ever seen you and you'll be hitchhiking to West Virginia. Do you understand?"

Yes, I did understand. All her talk in the beginning about making fans happy with visits from Kari wasn't true. She'd hired me for the money I could bring in, and that was all.

She sent me a challenging gaze. "Since you obviously feel you're ready for your role as Kari, you won't mind that I added a couple of appearances to your calendar next week."

I knew she expected me to protest, but I didn't. I was ready.

• • •

We flew out to San Antonio the next day, barely speaking to each other. I didn't tell her about the pictures the paparazzi had taken or the things I'd talked about with Grant. I didn't want to give her any other reasons to yell at me because if she did, I'd probably quit on the spot. And I didn't want to quit.

I had six weeks left until I met my father. And I admit I got a thrill from all the attention I received as a celebrity.

But I also wanted to do this for Kari. The memory of her falling apart, sliding to the floor when she learned Lorna planned on exposing her gambling debt—I'd never seen anyone so upset before. She was my sister, and I wanted to fix it for her. If her debts were paid, there wouldn't be anything scandalous to write about.

When I got situated in the hotel in San Antonio, I texted Kari a long message telling her I was worried about her. I put in links to gambling support groups. I half expected her to get angry at me for suggesting it, but she wrote back, "Don't stress about it. I'm fine. It's just money."

It's just money. What would it be like to have that attitude? Money was never "just money" to me. It was time, effort, opportunity, acceptance, and power. It was not printed with George Washington's and Abraham Lincoln's faces, but with my mother's face, bent over the kitchen table paying bills.

Kari and I kept texting back and forth. Maren had already told her I'd gone to the hospital, and she wrote, "Thanks for doing that. Now those hospital people will stop thinking I'm totally heartless."

Which made me even madder at Maren for getting in my face and yelling about it. Kari had been happy I'd done it.

I left out the part about the paparazzi and duet request, but texted her that Grant was finding out more about Lorna's book, which made her so happy she called to get the details.

"Let me know as soon as you hear from him," she said. "My lawyer says the more information we have about what's in that book, the easier it will be to stop it before it goes to press."

"I'll keep you updated," I said.

She let out a sympathetic sigh. "I'm sorry you have to deal with Grant. I know what a pain he is."

Without trying, I could conjure up Grant's square jaw and flawless features . . . the rich sound of his laugh. "He's not really such a jerk."

There was a pause, then she said, "Oooh," making the word sound like it had traversed a hill. "Well, it still would never work out between us, so you can't encourage him."

"I know. I told him Michael and I were just taking a break."

"Right," she said. "And I'm hoping our break will be over soon. Michael sent me three hundred roses yesterday. Isn't that so romantic? He's coming over soon."

"Congratulations," I said. I couldn't manage to muster much enthusiasm, though. I wondered what Grant would think when the tabloids reported that Kari and Michael were back together again.

• • •

Maren booked me to do a few songs at the San Antonio stock and rodeo show, but she didn't go with me. Someone from the organization was in charge of picking me and my entourage up, seeing to any needs I had, and returning us to the hotel. No one ever saw Maren. If I was caught, I already knew she would deny having any part or knowledge of this scheme.

I was fine through wardrobe, makeup, and getting my hair glitterfied. I was confident, even. But when I saw the stage and got a glimpse of the audience, I froze up. I nearly couldn't do it. I had expected hundreds of people, but about three thousand people sat in the stands.

How could I walk out there and lie to all of those people about who I was? What if something went wrong and I couldn't pull this off? I had spent so much time practicing the dance moves—what if I forgot the words and everyone figured out I was lip-synching? Would they boo me off the stage?

Maren had assured me I was only doing small concerts for Kari, and while I waited to go on, I called her to discuss her definition of the word *small*. She spent the next five minutes giving me a pep talk about how I was like a mall Santa Claus talking to children at Christmas. It didn't matter that Santa wasn't real. It made the children happy to meet him. Did I want to deny people Santa? That's what I'd be doing if I didn't go out there.

I wondered if a mall Santa had ever been dragged away in handcuffs and charged for fraud, but I didn't ask.

My legs shook as I walked out on the stage, and I had to force myself to keep moving. The crowd, however, cheered before the music even started. Every face I saw brimmed with excitement. Their admiration triggered something in me—adrenaline, energy, hope. I went through the first song tense, but without any mistakes. I messed up a move in the second song, but no one seemed to notice or care. They liked me even though I wasn't perfect. That's when I relaxed and had fun being the center of attention. I put a little bit of extra flair in my dance moves. I panned for the cameras, flipping my hair around until glitter flew over the stage. It looked like Tinker Bell had stopped by. I finished the last song out of breath and with my heart pounding—and was sorry the concert had ended. Every clap of applause felt like an "I love you" thrown to me.

The next day we flew to Florida for the Strawberry Festival and another small concert. I tried to explain to Maren that she couldn't call it "a small concert" if the number of people who came could conceivably overthrow a third-world dictatorship. Which caused a lot of eye rolling on her part, and she pointedly called them "shorter concerts" after that.

I was dying to tell Lori about meeting Grant, but I couldn't. Our phone conversations mostly consisted of her filling me in on any high school drama and me making up stories about hanging out at the beach. "Most days I'm covered in sand," I told her.

It wasn't sand, though. It was glitter. It found its way into my suitcases, my normal clothes, and the sheets of my hotel beds. That's when I really learned that all that glitters isn't gold. Some of it is just tiny annoying golden squares that poke into you.

After Florida, I went to Denver to lip-synch the national anthem at a pro hockey game. When we flew back to California Thursday night, I felt like I'd been living on nerves and adrenaline all week.

While out on the road, I had called my mom to talk about Larry. "Abuela says you're dating him because you think I need a father figure in my life."

Mom gave a disgruntled humph. "That's just because Abuela can't fathom why else I'd be dating him."

"Well, Abuela has a point."

"Larry is a very considerate man," Mom said. "And he's dependable." She didn't add anything else to the list, and I wondered if this was the sum total of his good characteristics.

"You're not getting serious about him, are you?"

"He wants to get serious, but I haven't decided yet," she said.

"Well, just don't make any big decisions until I get home, okay?"

"Fine," she said, "then don't stay away too long."

I found that statement chilling even after I hung up the phone.

CHAPTER 10

On Friday morning Grant called to say he had a copy of Lorna's book. He figured I already had plans for the evening but wondered if I could meet somewhere for lunch. "A professional lunch," he said, as though I would have turned him down otherwise.

I didn't turn him down. I wanted to read what the book said about both my father and Kari. Despite Maren's assertions that Kari only suffered from bad budgeting, I worried about her. I told Grant I'd meet him at the restaurant.

Maren had relaxed my schedule since I'd returned from my events. I still had dancing, exercising sessions, and studying to do, but my afternoons were free. Maren was spending the day arranging details of Kari's mega concert in San Diego and had told me that as a reward for my hard work I could go shopping. In fact, she'd left a list of acceptable and unacceptable places.

The restaurant, I noted, was not on the unacceptable list, therefore I technically wasn't disobeying her by going. And the nice thing about living with Maren was that she didn't have paparazzi circling her home. Anyone who was looking for Kari would be camped out by her house.

I called Bao-Zhi to pick me up, texted Kari that I was getting the book from Grant, and headed off.

This time, Grant had purposely chosen an elite restaurant where we could go in through a back door to a private room so we didn't have to worry about the paparazzi. I'd only been a celebrity for a few days and already I hated them for making my life more complicated.

I told Bao-Zhi he didn't have to wait for me while I ate; I'd call him when I needed him. I told myself I'd done this because I hated wasting Bao-Zhi's time. It had nothing to do with the fact that I noticed Grant's green Jaguar in the parking lot, or that I wanted to prolong my time with him.

Before I'd even gotten out of my car, a guy in a tuxedo came out of the restaurant to greet me. He took me upstairs to a private room overlooking the city. Grant was already there, sitting at the table. Just seeing him, gorgeousness personified, nearly made me stumble. What was God thinking when he created a guy this handsome? He wasn't a gift to womankind, he was a torture device. I shouldn't be required to look at him when I could never have him.

He smiled, and my heart constricted into a tight knot. I sat down and smiled back.

He slid a two-inch stack of paper to my side of the table. "Here's what Lorna's written so far. She's still researching a few of the chapters, so there are some gaps."

He leaned back in his chair, and I tried not to stare at every movement his broad shoulders made. "I read it last night," he said.

I skimmed the introduction, which was the story of

Kari's firing Lorna because Lorna had tried to help the hospital director do a benefit concert for sick children. I hadn't gotten far when I let out a sigh of disgust. "This is awful."

"Which part?"

"The woman doesn't know how to write. On the first page it says, 'Caring for no one, the benefit for sick children was turned down.' Besides the fact that it makes it sound like the benefit cared for no one, the sentence is in passive voice and has a dangling modifier. This sentence alone would raise an English teacher's blood pressure to dangerous levels."

Grant picked up his water glass and took a sip. "That's what bothers you? The dangling modifier in that sentence?"

"Well, I expected the rest to be bad." I let out a sigh and read on about how Lorna had interviewed several people, etc., etc., and did all sorts of meticulous research.

I moved on to the first chapter, entitled "A Princess Is Born." It told the story of how Alex Kingsley lost his young wife while out on tour. "His guilt and sorrow overwhelmed him for years," Lorna wrote. "He compensated by lavishing gifts on his daughter. In terms of toys and clothes, young Kari had double anything she ever wanted, including a slew of nannies, a child-sized Hummer, a personal swimming pool, and a Shetland pony."

It went on cataloging his excesses and told how he threw himself into his work. He came out with four albums in five years. He took Kari and her nanny on tour with him when she was young, some years doing as many as 125 concerts. "Kari learned from the time she was small," Lorna wrote, "that the only important life was a life onstage."

A picture of the two of them was included in the text. Kari looked to be about four years old. She wore a cowboy hat, ruffled skirt, and rhinestone boots. He held her up for a crowd to see.

I stared at it and tears pressed against my eyes. The words blurred together and I didn't even know why I was crying. Was it because I was jealous of the time and attention Kari got from the father I never knew, or the fact that he was so overwhelmed by sorrow and guilt he had wanted to buy for her what she couldn't have, a mother?

I didn't notice that Grant had come around the table to sit beside me until he spoke. "Maybe this isn't a good idea. You're already crying, and you're not even to the bad stuff. Why don't you read it later?"

But I didn't want to wait. "I'll be okay."

I wasn't okay. I got to the sentence, "Friends tried to convince Alex to remarry, but his answer was always the same: He'd already proved he didn't make a good husband." And I cried all over again. This time I knew why. I cried for my mother and her dreams that didn't happen, that couldn't have happened because she'd pinned them on somebody too broken and unattainable to love her back.

Grant slid the manuscript away from me. "Look, this kind of stuff is said about celebrities all the time. People don't believe half of it, and they don't care about the rest. Even if it does go to press, you're not going to lose any fans over this stupid book."

I nodded, but the tears came anyway. I hated that I'd become so emotional here in California. I hadn't cried this much over my father since elementary school, when I first realized I could never go to the donuts-for-dads-and-kids breakfasts they put on once a year.

Grant slid his arm around me, and I laid my head against his shoulder. I shouldn't have leaned into him that way, but I couldn't help myself. I wanted the comfort.

He said, "Really, don't worry about it. A tabloid once said my songs had subliminal messages that brainwashed kids so they'd do whatever I asked. Apparently I'm trying to take over the free world with an army of junior high zombies." He ran his hand through the ends of my hair, loosely winding his fingers through it. "I had it framed and sent to my high school civics teacher. She thought I'd never paid attention to any of her lectures on government."

I laughed even though I was still crying, but I couldn't speak. I grabbed my napkin from the table and used it to dab the tears off my face. You spend that much time buffing, concealing, and bronzing your skin and you don't want it ruined by one outburst. "It's just hard to read about my father." I could tell Grant didn't understand, so I added, "Things are distant between us right now, but I don't want them to be. At least I don't think I want them to be. That's part of the problem—I don't know—and I want to talk to him, but I'm afraid to. I don't know what he'll say. I don't even know if he wants me in his life."

Somewhere in that I'd quit being Kari and had become Alexia. My mom had said she hadn't told me Alex Kingsley was my father because she didn't want me to be devastated if he rejected me. It seemed like a cop-out answer at the time, but now that I was here in California, counting down the days until I met him, I realized my mother was right.

"Of course your dad wants you in his life," Grant said. And then he pulled me even closer. I let my head fall against his shoulder and stayed there listening to him breathe, feeling the slow rise and release of his chest. Neither of us moved for a long time.

Finally he said, "Can I ask you a question?"

"Yeah."

"Do you promise you'll be honest?"

"No."

He laughed and I liked the feel of it against my cheek.

"It depends on what you ask," I said.

"Do you really have a gambling problem?"

I sat up away from him, but not very far away. He still had his arm around my shoulders. I wanted to answer for me, but knew I had to answer for Kari. "I hope I don't anymore. I worked this whole week doing concerts to pay off debts. Really, that's the honest answer. I could show you my latest dance routine to 'Two Hearts Apart' right now to prove it."

"I'll pass on that." His hand returned to my hair, flipping

it lazily between his fingers. "Do you really have temper tantrums when you're upset?"

He was asking about Kari. But with his arm around me and the smell of his cologne encircling me, I couldn't be Kari. I relaxed back into him. "I don't have *tantrums.* Well, I did push Theresa Davidson into a cafeteria garbage can when I was eleven. And there was an incident not too long ago involving some books that ended up on the floor. But I'm doing my best to reform. That's the honest answer."

"One more question." His fingers were still intertwined in my hair. His gaze settled on my eyes. "Is there any chance the two of us could be more than friends?"

I didn't answer for a full minute. I just looked at the table and felt the heat of his arm draped around my shoulders. Finally I said, "I still consider Michael my boyfriend."

Grant didn't move. Neither did I.

"You didn't say that was the honest answer," he said.

"I know."

He shifted his weight to look at me better. His eyes were serious, smoldering. Then his gaze slid downward, stopping at my lips. He leaned forward, about to kiss me. I should have moved, turned away, said something. But I didn't.

Then the waiter came in. "Oh," he said, looking back and forth between us with obvious discomfort. "Do you need more time to order?"

Grant straightened up, picked up his menu, and glanced over it. "Porterhouse steak. Medium rare." He handed his menu to the waiter and turned his attention back to me.

"Do you know what you want?" Only the way he said it made me think he wasn't talking about lunch.

I peered at the menu, but my heart was beating too fast and it made it hard to concentrate on the words. "Sorry," I said to the waiter. "I'm searching for something that's vegetarian."

He rattled off a few items, which I also had a hard time concentrating on.

Grant made a pondering "hmmm" sound, and I glanced back at him. His eyes glinted wickedly. "Are you sure you don't want to cheat?" And that time for sure he wasn't talking about lunch.

"Cheating is bad," I said.

"You're right." He sent a killer smile in my direction. "I don't want you to cheat. I want you to change your mind altogether. Choose something that's better for you."

I handed the menu back to the waiter. "Sorry, I'm not going to cheat today. I'll have the vegetable lasagna."

Grant shook his head in mock disappointment—or maybe it was real disappointment; it was hard to tell since he was still smiling—but he didn't bring the subject of us up again.

We spent the rest of lunch discussing things like where we'd like to travel. He had actual plans. I had dreams I passed off as plans. He asked me what my favorite natural wonder was, and I said, "The ocean."

"I don't think that's technically a natural wonder."

"It is to me. I love swimming in the waves."

"I meant like the Grand Canyon."

Without thinking about it, I said, "I've never been there."

I realized this was a mistake when his eyes widened. "You've never been to the Grand Canyon?"

Kari probably had, but I couldn't take it back now, so I shrugged. "I'm too busy to take the time out for that sort of thing."

He shook his head in disbelief. I knew I needed to change the topic of conversation. "So what were your favorite subjects in school?"

"School?" He leaned back in his chair as though he needed the extra space to think about it. "Probably math. It always made sense. Unlike English, economics, and girls."

"And exactly how do you plan on taking over the free world if you don't understand economics?"

"I'll hire advisers. I'll hire you, in fact."

"Okay. Let me know when your army of junior high zombies is ready."

I didn't want lunch to end. I ordered a fudge brownie sundae for dessert, even though I wasn't hungry anymore and Maren wouldn't approve of me eating something dripping with calories. I just wanted to prolong the time I spent with him.

But finally even that disappeared and then I didn't have a reason to keep him any longer. We both stood up and he said, "I'll walk you to your car."

"I had my driver drop me off," I said. "I'll give him a call."

"Oh, then I'll take you home," Grant said.

In retrospect the problem was that being with Grant made it hard to think straight. When I asked if he knew how to get to my house and he said yes, I didn't think anything more of it. He'd already taken me to Maren's before, which of course was where I needed to go. I was so wrapped up in talking to him that I didn't realize he'd driven to Kari's house until we went up the drive and he asked for the gate code. Then he said, "Oh, never mind. It looks like we're following the pool truck. Do you have a nice pool?"

Probably. Unless pool trucks came to houses for other reasons. I smiled over at him. "It's okay."

Then I took deep breaths, suddenly realizing that the next few minutes could go very bad in a lot of ways. "How did you know where I lived?" I asked, doing my best to keep my voice at a normal pitch.

"When Lorna first came down to the hospital after you'd fired her, I drove her up here to talk to you. You weren't home, though." He glanced over at me and smiled. "I wonder what would have happened if we'd met then? Do you think things would have turned out differently?"

Oh, yeah. They would have turned out very differently. The real Kari would have turned the hose on them. Then at the club, Grant would have seen that I was a fake from the start. But I shrugged like it was one of those unknowable mysteries and scanned the yard and trees to make sure Kari wasn't out for a stroll.

Thankfully, I didn't see her.

The pool truck stopped by the house. Were they going to ring the doorbell? Would Kari come out to talk to them?

Grant pulled up near the garage and stopped the car. I didn't move. I just stared at the yard trying to think of any plausible excuse for why we should leave immediately.

An older Latino man got out of the pool truck. He hefted a toolbox and a jug out of his truck bed, then walked around to the back of the house.

I couldn't even tell if Kari was home right now. Who knew whether her car was in the four-car garage. Really, her house had a four-car garage. Like maybe her Porsche wanted to have slumber parties. Grant got out of the car, but I still didn't move. My muscles had completely stopped working. What if she'd seen us pull up and came to one of the front windows to see who it was?

Apparently Grant thought I was waiting for him to open my door, because that's what he did. I got out and scanned the house windows as we walked to the front door. Nothing. I opened my purse and fumbled through it until we reached the doorstep. "I, uh—this is really embarrassing. I don't have my house keys with me. But I know my assistant has an extra copy. I'll give her a call and she can—"

Grant leaned over and tried the doorknob. It swung open. "You're in luck. You also forgot to lock the door."

"Oh," I said. "Great." How come Kari never locked her doors? Didn't she know that was unsafe? I looked inside. No sign of Kari. I stepped through the doorway. I had told her I was getting the manuscript, so she might not be surprised to see me at her house, but she would definitely be surprised to see Grant. And he would be really surprised to see her. "Thanks for lunch, and for the manuscript. I'll, um—"

He let out a sigh and stepped inside after me. "Look, we need to talk. You know, about what happened at lunch. Or at least what I wanted to happen at lunch. Despite what you said about Michael, I think you wanted it to happen too."

What was I supposed to say to that? I opened my mouth and nothing came out. Then I heard footsteps clicking on the tile off in the left side of the house coming toward us.

CHAPTER 11

I grabbed Grant's hand and pulled him off toward the right side of the house. "Do you want a drink or something?" I asked. "Let's go to the kitchen." We walked through a sitting room with a bay window that faced the front lawn. "This is my reading room," I guessed. "It's where I go over my fan mail." It had two doors. I took him through the one in the back, and we walked into a room full of shelves holding porcelain dolls and curios. "And this is my, um, doll collection room, and you can see I also have lots of ceramic cats because, hey, you can never have too many of those."

The room was a dead end. I towed him back into the sitting room. He raised an eyebrow at me questioningly, but he didn't come right out and ask if I was lost in my own house. "I thought you'd like a tour while you're here," I said, by way of explanation. "I don't get many visitors, so I like to show the place off when I can." Then I pulled him through the other sitting room door. We went into a hallway. I didn't hear Kari coming up behind us, but that didn't mean we wouldn't run into her at any moment. I glanced into a doorway but didn't go inside. "That's my den," I said.

He looked inside to be polite. "Nice."

I pulled him farther down the hallway. "Here's my guest bedroom." We walked a few more feet. "And another guest bedroom." Then we reached the end of the hallway and two doorways on either side. "And here are two more guest bedrooms."

He peered into each one. "For someone who doesn't have a lot of visitors, you certainly have a lot of places to put them."

"Well, you can only fill so many rooms with ceramic cats."

"Are you avoiding talking about us?"

I pulled him back down the hallway. "No, not at all. Well, maybe a little bit." Where was the stupid kitchen? I was making enough noise that Kari would either know to stay out of my way, or come after me wielding a can of mace. Or maybe in a house this big she still didn't even know anyone had come inside. Would she scream if she suddenly saw us? And how exactly would I explain a screaming look-alike in my house?

I made it back to the first hallway and went the opposite direction this time. It opened up into a large family room complete with Roman-style columns and arched ceiling. Vases full of Michael's three hundred red roses stood on the coffee table, end tables, everywhere. I spotted the kitchen on the other side of the room, and the counters were covered too.

"So I take it you like red roses," Grant said.

"Yeah." I didn't offer any other explanation as I towed Grant into the kitchen. "I'm not sure what I have around to drink," I said, and then ran into my next problem. I didn't know where the glasses were, and what was worse, I didn't see a refrigerator anywhere. Rows of cherrywood cupboards and cabinets surrounded us, and a huge island with a black granite top sat in the middle of the room. But she had to have a fridge somewhere in here, didn't she? Everybody has a fridge. I turned around once, then twice, but didn't see it. Was it in a different room altogether?

He took a step toward me and tilted his head, reading my expression. "Am I making you nervous?"

"No, no. I had the maid rearrange everything, and I can't remember where I told her to put the glasses."

He walked over and took my hand. "You don't have to get me anything to drink. I just want to talk to you."

"Okay." It wasn't really okay, though. Holding his hand made my heart race, and I had to tell him I wanted Michael to be my boyfriend, which would be hard to make convincing when I'd nearly kissed Grant in the restaurant. Would he think I was a hypocrite or just a tease?

I forced myself to look into his blue eyes and tried not to get pulled into their depths. I had to be strong. Kari wanted Michael, so that was that. Alexia Garcia didn't have a choice in the matter. Someone like Grant would never be interested in a poor girl from West Virginia.

Then I heard footsteps again, this time coming toward the kitchen.

I looked outside through the sliding glass door to where a huge pool sprawled in the backyard. "Let's talk outside." I pulled him that way, tugging at the sliding glass door until it opened.

We stepped outside into the warm air, and I slid the door shut. This, I realized, was the perfect solution to my problem. When Kari walked by and saw us out here, the closed door would muffle her startled scream or angry gasp—or whatever was the normal reaction to finding your double hanging out with another teen idol by your pool. If I kept Grant's attention on me, he wouldn't look back into the house. And once Kari realized we were out here, she'd know she had to keep herself hidden until Grant left.

I strolled a few feet toward the pool. As far as pools went, it was spectacular. Hewn stones surrounded the water, like the earth had cracked open to create a lake for her. Waterfalls flowed on both sides, and a large Jacuzzi bubbled in the corner. One of the waterfalls only let out a trickle of water, though, and the pool man stood beside it, watching it with dissatisfaction.

Grant noticed him. "Are you sure this is the best place for us to talk?"

But I wasn't about to take Grant back inside while Kari was roaming around her house. "I'll tell the pool man he can leave," I said. I left Grant and walked toward the older man. I didn't get too close, in case he could tell the difference between Kari and me. "Pardon me, can you come back and do that another time?"

The pool man looked past me to Grant, and then nodded.

He spoke with a strong accent, so I knew English wasn't his first language. "Okay. If you want, I come back tomorrow. I fix the chlorine level for you then too. It's okay?"

"Yes. Thank you very much."

The pool man picked up his toolbox and a jug of chemicals, then walked around the side of the house. I motioned Grant to follow me to a couple of padded wicker chairs. I sat on one. He sat on the other.

"Now we can talk," I told him.

He put his elbows on his knees and leaned toward me. I noticed how the light glinted off his brown hair and how his blue eyes looked a shade lighter out in the sunshine. "I know this is unexpected for both of us," he said. "If someone had told me two weeks ago that Kari Kingsley was my type, I wouldn't have believed them. But now that I've gotten to know you, well, you're nothing like I thought. You're smart and funny, and you were so good with the kids at the hospital. The staff is getting tired of hearing your CD, by the way. It's all the kids want to play now. They told me to ask you when your next CD is coming out."

"Not soon enough to save their sanity."

He smiled and took hold of my hand, gently caressing my fingers. "I want to get to know you better. I think both of us would like that."

I would have answered him, but the pool man came back around the house, walking in quick, angry strides to the waterfall.

"I thought you were leaving," I called to him.

He didn't look at me. He let his toolbox thunk to the ground and knelt beside the valve box. "I go to my truck, and you yell at me for not finishing the job. So now I finish the job. I fix the waterfall, then I adjust the chlorine so it not burn your eyes." He flipped open the valve box, took out a wrench, and twisted something viciously.

Grant looked at the pool man, then back at me questioningly.

I lowered my voice and shrugged. "He has a drinking problem, but, well, I keep him around because he's getting help."

"We can go back inside," Grant said.

I shook my head, and this time I switched to Spanish when I spoke to the pool man. "I'm really sorry to keep asking you to leave. I can't explain myself to you, but go back to your truck, and if I yell at you again for leaving, remind me that I have a visitor by the pool—a visitor I need to be discreet about."

The pool man stopped mid twist and stared at me. "You speak Spanish?" he asked.

"Yes," I said.

"Okay," he said, and then in Spanish added, "And, uh, I'm sorry about those things my men said when they came to clean your pool. They didn't know you could understand."

He picked up his toolbox, still apologizing about whatever his workers had said, then waved good-bye in my direction and went around the side of the house.

When I turned back to Grant, he eyed me in surprise. "I

thought you couldn't speak Spanish. It's there in chapter one—your dad never exposed you to your cultural roots."

"He didn't. That doesn't mean no one did, though." I should have shrugged and told him, "Well, you can't believe everything in Lorna's book." But it was getting harder to lie to him. I changed the subject before he could ask further questions about where I'd learned Spanish. "Anyway, where were we before that interruption?"

"You were telling me that you were going to dump Michael and give us a chance."

I smiled at him. "I don't think I said that."

"You were thinking it, though. I could tell."

Maybe I was thinking it, but I couldn't say it. I gazed at the sky, gathering strength, enjoying this last moment before everything turned awkward between us. Finally I turned to him again, looking at eyes that were the same color as the sky.

He grinned and waited for my answer.

I said, "You've never had a girl turn you down in your life, have you?"

"Nope." He ran his thumb lazily across my fingers. "Don't break my streak."

He said this so casually, so confidently, offering more proof that celebrities lived above the rest of us, getting whatever they wanted and choosing when to love and when to discard us. "You've *never* had a girl turn you down?"

He shrugged. "There was Hayley Powell in the first grade.

I asked her to marry me and she stuck her tongue out. Put me right off proposing."

"Hmmm," I said, trying to sound analytical. This was hard to do. He pulled my hand toward him, making me lean closer.

The jangling of the toolbox broke into the moment. The pool man stormed back over to the valve box, dropping his toolbox with a dramatic clank. "I taking care of the water-fall now!" he yelled. "You see? So now you no play your little games. It's because Enrique said, *'Ella cree que su caca no huele.'* This is why you are trying to make me *loco*, no?"

In Spanish I said, "Didn't you explain—"

"Yes, I explain," he said. "But then you told me you no speak Spanish."

Oh. I guess I should have mentioned that he'd have to speak to Kari in English.

I turned back to Grant. "I think he's off his medication. Maybe we should let him finish and have this conversation another time."

I motioned to get up, but Grant squeezed my hand and lowered his voice. "We don't have to wait for another time. Just say yes."

"Yes to what?"

"Yes to us."

I leaned closer, keeping my gaze on his hands so I didn't have to meet his eyes. "It's not that easy. Things are complicated right now, complicated in ways I can't explain. But I do like you—I'm telling the truth about that. It's just that there are—" I glanced up and saw Kari standing behind the glass door, mouth open, hands on her hips, staring at us. Grant's back was to her. But when he saw my startled expression, he turned his head, following my gaze.

"Grant!" I called, yanking his attention back to me.

"What?" he asked.

I had to do something. I couldn't let him turn around again. So I leaned all the way into him, putting my knee on his chair to keep my balance. I took hold of his shoulders and kissed him. And not lightly—this was a don't-you-dare-open-your-eyes, full-on kiss.

Only I kept *my* eyes open because Kari was mouthing, "What are you doing?"

With one hand I waved in Kari's direction, telling her to go away, since I really couldn't say anything at that point. But I stopped waving when Grant wrapped his arms around my back.

Kari glared at me, then turned on her heel and flounced out of sight. She wasn't happy about this, but at least she knew to keep hidden until Grant left.

Which meant I could stop kissing Grant now. Only, the feel of his hands moving slowly down my back made my heart ricochet in my chest. I didn't want to move. I shut my eyes, relaxed into him, and didn't end the kiss for several more moments. When I finally did sit back in my chair, I could only stare at him, breathing hard. I didn't know what to say.

"I take it that was a yes," he said.

That would be the foregone conclusion, wouldn't it? How could I say no now? I looked at the empty sliding glass door. "We'll have to be discreet. No one can know about this. No one can see us together."

"Right," he said. "Let the paparazzi harass someone else for a while."

I'd completely forgotten about the pool man until he called over, "I'm done now. Everything is okay." Then he waved his wrench at me with a sly smile. "I understand now why I think I go crazy. I see the two of you together. . . ." He apparently couldn't come up with the word for twins in English, so he said it in Spanish. "*Gemelas.*" Then he headed back around the side of the house, this time with an easy, confident gait.

Grant watched him go. "Gemelas?"

"Gemini," I said. "You know—the astrological sign." Which strictly speaking is true. Gemini is the sign of the twins.

"Geminis drive him crazy?" Grant blinked in confusion. "I'm an Aries."

I shrugged. "Some people just don't make a lot of sense."

He took my hand, as though it wasn't worth figuring out, and then he kissed me again.

My heart somersaulted in my chest. Maybe I could make this work. Maybe I could find a way to be with him so he'd never figure out the truth. Or maybe after I was sure he liked the real me—not Kari—I could tell him the truth about everything. There were too many maybes scurrying around like mice underfoot, but they were all I had.

He leaned away from me, smiling.

I smiled back at him. "I wish you could stay for a while, but I've got a full schedule this afternoon."

"That's okay," he said. "We can get together tomorrow, or the next day. When do you have some free time?"

I stood up and glanced at the sliding door. Still clear. "I'll check my schedule and call you." Now that I had my afternoons free, I should be able to see him without Maren knowing. He stood up and we held hands as we walked back through the house—this time thankfully without getting lost.

He kissed me one last time in the entryway, then we said good-bye and I shut the door. As soon as I did, Kari walked into the entryway, her hands on her hips. "That was completely revolting. I can't believe I just saw myself make out with Grant Delray."

"Sorry," I said, even though I wasn't—well, I wasn't sorry about the kissing, anyway.

"You know, when you said you'd bring the book over, I didn't realize you meant you were bringing my archnemesis too."

"That was an accident. He wanted to take me home, and I didn't realize he knew where you lived. So then he came inside because he wanted to talk—and by the way, how come you don't have a refrigerator in your kitchen? You have four guest bedrooms and a ceramic cat shrine, but no refrigerator?"

"I have a fridge. It's a built-in."

I had no idea what she meant. "A built-in what?"

She let out a sigh. "It has wood paneling on it so it blends in with the cabinets."

Which seemed pointless: camouflage fridges. "You're kidding me."

"A lot of upscale kitchens have them." She put one hand on her hip. "Did you get a copy of Lorna's book?"

I nodded toward the antique chest, where I'd left it when I came in. I'd wanted to read it before I gave it to Kari, but now that she'd seen it, I wouldn't be able to pry it out of her hands.

She picked it up and flipped through some of the pages. "This is great! I'm telling Maren to give you a bonus for this."

"Thanks," I said, but I didn't mean it. Suddenly I felt like I'd used Grant.

She flipped through a few more pages, a look of icy determination on her face. "Now that we've got this, we don't need Grant anymore. You'll have to break it off with him. I *so* don't want a relationship with him."

I didn't answer, but she didn't seem to notice. She walked toward the living room. "I'm going to read this right now."

I followed after her. "I probably should know what's in it too. It's research. You can hand me the pages after you're done reading them."

Which is how we ended up sitting on her couch most of the afternoon reading the book assembly-line fashion. She didn't have much reaction to the stuff about our father, but I read and reread it. He'd taken Kari to Hawaii for an entire summer when she was seven. I would have been almost five at the time and living in a rundown apartment complex with no yard to play in.

The really chilling part of the manuscript was that Lorna had made a notation in chapter one that her interview with Alex Kingsley's then manager was still pending. I stared at that sentence for minutes, letting the other pages pile up on the couch beside me. My mother had called his manager and told him she was pregnant. Would he remember that? Would he mention it?

Finally I went on to Kari's later years, which included quotes from prep school friends. Well, perhaps *friends* isn't the right word. Friends wouldn't have said that kind of stuff about her. I imagined Lorna had found Kari's version of the Cliquistas and interviewed them. I could tell every time Kari read a new story. She'd gasp and let out a high-pitched squeaky noise. Sometimes she'd yell, "That is so not true!" Or "Anybody would have thrown something after *People* magazine said their evening gown looked like a pile of window treatment samples come to life." She also swore a lot, despite that whole thing about being a role model for young girls.

The book said that as a teenager Kari had had drinking binges, that she'd go on daylong shopping sprees, and that after her comment about not doing anything to be green because she didn't celebrate Saint Patrick's Day, she'd refused to go out in public for two months. The book also talked about the guys in her life: rock stars, television actors, athletes. It made me wonder about Grant's expectations for a girlfriend.

I put the manuscript down in my lap. "Kari, would you ever date someone who wasn't a celebrity?"

She kept her attention on the paper in front of her. "Of course. A guy doesn't have to be famous to hang out with me as long as, you know, he's really rich or powerful."

"You wouldn't ever date a normal guy?"

She shrugged. "What would be the point in that?"

"Maybe you had a lot in common."

"Not if he's not rich or famous."

Oh. I went back to the manuscript, reading it less carefully now and wondering if Grant would have answered the same way.

We were about done with the manuscript when the front door opened and a male voice yelled, "Kari?"

CHAPTER 12

Kari and I looked at each other. "Grant came back," I said. "Hide."

She shook her head. "That's Michael. You're the one who needs to hide." She looked toward the sound. "At least I think that's Michael."

We both stood up. Neither of us answered him.

A bubble of panic pushed against my chest. What were we supposed to do when neither of us knew who was in the house? "Why don't you ever lock your front door?" I asked.

"You used it last," she said. "You didn't lock it either."

"Kari?" the voice came again, this time closer. "Are you home?"

"Michael," we both said at once.

"Just a second!" she called back, which she shouldn't have done because then footsteps headed in our direction.

I didn't have much time. I looked around, trying to remember which doorways led where. Could I make it out of the sliding glass door? No. Would he hear my footsteps if I ran across the tile? Kari whispered, "Hide! Hide!" while shaking her hands.

I ducked behind the couch, then heard him come into the room. From my place on the floor, I saw a pair of brown loafers. No discernible socks.

"Kari," he said, turning the word into an exclamation of happiness. I could picture him, even though I couldn't see him. I'd seen his soap opera—he played a brooding bad boy whose dark bangs constantly draped over one eye. That way he could brush his hair away every five minutes and shoot dramatic, sizzling looks at the camera.

Kari's black shoes joined his on the floor. I could tell they were hugging. "Hey, sweetie."

"I love what you've done to the place," he said. "A floral shop motif."

"Thanks again for the flowers."

Silence. I could tell they were kissing.

Get him out of here, I thought. *Take him by the hand and lead him anywhere else.*

Although Kari and I look like twins, apparently we don't have that psychic twin connection. After another minute of kissing, Kari said, "So what brings you here?"

"I had to see the most beautiful girl in the world."

More giggling from Kari. Probably more kissing too.

"So what's with the paper on the couch?" Michael asked.

Kari at last seemed to remember I was in the room because she said, "Oh, it's nothing. Just a book. Let's go outside."

"A book?" Michael asked. "Are you writing one?" Instead of leaving, Michael walked over to the couch. I held my breath and tried to shrink into the floor tile. I heard the shuffling of paper. "What kind of book is this?"

"A bad one. Lorna Beck is bashing me."

"You're kidding." He sat down. The couch jiggled. "Can she do that legally?"

The couch jiggled again and I knew Kari had joined him. "My lawyer is trying to stop her." She let out an aggravated sigh. "See, this is the problem with hiring poor people to work for you: They don't care if you sue them. What do they have to lose? Lorna drives a Kia, for heaven's sake. Like I'd want *that* in a settlement."

I heard more shuffling of paper. Michael said, "Does she mention me?"

"Yeah. She says I keep driving you away with my temper."

He let out a scoffing grunt. "And I always thought it was the way you keep flirting with other guys."

"Exactly," Kari said. "Lorna doesn't know what she's talking about."

"I want to read it," he said, and the only sound for a while was papers turning, unless you count the sound of my muscles hardening into knots as I tried not to move or breathe loudly.

Finally Kari said, "I'm thirsty. Can you grab me some orange juice and I'll keep searching through the pages?"

"Sure thing." He stood and his shoes went toward the kitchen. Kari fluttered a hand over the back of the couch, as though I might not have realized Michael had left. I slipped off my shoes so they wouldn't clomp against the tile and tiptoed to what I thought was a way out of the room—but that turned out to be just an alcove with a window seat. Kari's guitar lay on top of composition paper. I turned around to leave, but then heard Michael's footsteps coming back to the couch.

So I pressed myself against the wall. I was trapped, but at least not visible. Michael could see the wall opposite me, but not where I stood.

Which was good news, until I realized that a huge mirror hung across from me. I could see the two of them framed perfectly: Michael pushing paper over to give himself a place to sit down. Kari taking the drink of orange juice from him.

I might have made a noise at that point. Maybe said something very un-role-modelish. Michael looked over. His eyes connected with mine through the mirror. I froze with dread. I'd been caught. Should I say something or let Kari come up with an explanation?

But Michael's gaze brushed past me and returned to Kari. "I like your new portrait in your writing nook."

Kari looked over at me then and was a lot less thrilled by the new portrait in her writing nook. She actually glared at me as though I'd done it on purpose. As though I'd said to myself, "Why leave when I could stand here and pretend to be a picture of Kari instead?"

But I did stand there, holding the same pose in case Michael glanced over at the mirror again. It was a good five minutes before Michael read the pages that Lorna had written about him and Kari could convince him that they needed to go outside to check on the pool.

I didn't wait to put my shoes back on after that. I rushed out of the room, fled down the hallway, and didn't stop running until I reached Kari's front gate. I called my driver to come get me, but my heart didn't stop pounding until I made it to Maren's house.

. . .

One of Kari's assistants dropped off the book for Maren the next morning. She read it while she ate breakfast. It was odd to see her calmly flipping through the pages as she ate her yogurt sprinkled with oat bran. I'd expected her to at least get a little defensive on Kari's behalf.

When I came back from my dance lesson, she'd not only finished the manuscript, she'd made copies. She put one into a manila envelope for Kari's lawyer and one into another envelope. Then she made a phone call. Her crisp professional voice changed, became more intimate and suddenly eager to please. I stayed in the kitchen taking slow sips from a water bottle so I could listen.

She talked about Lorna's book with more regret and emotion than she'd shown when she'd read it. "I'm sending a copy to her lawyer now," she said. "I'll send you one as well, if you like."

Who was she talking to? My father?

After a minute of silence she spoke again. "Well, despite that, I think I've really seen a turnaround. She's working hard, and she's sticking to a budget. She's a little behind on the album, but it's coming along."

The response to that, whatever it was, made Maren smile. "I take all the assignments you give me seriously, and besides, I adore Kari. I think she just needs a woman's influence in her life."

My fingers froze around my water bottle. It *was* him. My father was on the other end of that conversation. All the years of wanting him, of feeling abandoned, of wondering what he would say to me, suddenly sprang to the surface.

Maren went on cooing about what a wonderful girl Kari was, while I fought the urge to grab the phone out of her hand. That wouldn't be a normal thing to do. I did not want my father's first impression of me to be that I was a crazy person who burst into other people's conversations.

Still, I stared at Maren unwaveringly.

At last she said good-bye and slid her phone shut with a happy sigh. It was only then that she noticed my stare.

"That was Alex Kingsley, wasn't it?" I asked.

"Yes." Her voice returned to its normal businesslike tone. "I thought he should know about the book. After all, he's the star of chapter one."

I tried to make sense of the other things she'd said. "Did he ask you to straighten out Kari's financial affairs?"

She held up one hand like a teacher correcting a student. "Alex is simply a concerned father. Of course he wants me to help his daughter. However, you won't mention this conversation to Kari. I don't want her to think I'm helping her as a favor to him." And then she smiled again.

Too late. Kari already knew Maren was trying to make inroads with her father.

I watched as Maren slipped her cell phone back into a clip on her belt. She always wore it on her belt. And my father's number was on it.

I hadn't planned on calling him; I wanted to meet him face-to-face. Still, it was aggravating: my father was just a redial button away—and I still had no way to talk to him.

After my shower, I took the sapphire necklace and slipped it around my neck. I decided to wear it all the time. Perhaps it was an outside chance, but my father could stop by and see Maren sometime. If he did, I wanted to be ready.

· · ·

I spent the next week making appearances in Texas, Oklahoma, and New Mexico while Kari holed up at her house, writing and practicing songs. Maren came with me, and I noticed she never left her phone unattended. It stayed on her belt during the day, and she charged it in her hotel room at night. Once while we ate breakfast in the hotel, I pretended to be interested in upgrading my cell phone and came right out and asked her, "Can I see yours?"

She pressed her lips together in an unapologetic smile,

as though she enjoyed telling me no. "I never let anyone see it. It has private information."

So much for getting my father's number from her.

I thought about him a lot when I was out on the road performing. Being up on stage made me feel close to him. Sometimes when I was alone staring out a hotel window, he would come to mind, and my hand would reflexively go to the sapphire necklace around my throat.

I would think about his decisions, how so many decisions, really, affect more than the people who make them. Dwelling on this might make me responsible, or paralyzed, I wasn't sure which.

Luckily I wasn't alone very much. Some sort of assistant—either mine or people from whatever event I was doing—always seemed to hover around.

It was getting easier to play my role as Kari. I especially liked being gracious to all the staff I came in contact with: the tech people working on the sound systems and the spotlights, the ushers, the waiters, the hotel employees. I'd spent my life being one of the overlooked; I wanted to notice and thank them for their work now. And they were always so pleasantly surprised at how nice Kari Kingsley was.

Even when things went wrong that would have normally upset me—like when the sound system wasn't ready, thus causing one of my concerts to start twenty minutes late—I brushed it off. I didn't want to have a temper. That way no one could criticize my sister for being a prima donna.

Grant called every night while I was gone, which was always the highlight of my day. It wasn't the thunderous applause I got after a song, or the throngs of people giddy to see me. It was relaxing in my hotel room and Grant's voice on my phone that made my skin tingle. He made a date for the first day I was home and kept running ideas past me.

"Skydiving?" he'd ask. "Bungee jumping? How about running with the bulls in Pamplona?"

I kept telling him it didn't have to be anything elaborate. "Pizza and a DVD would be fine."

I knew I couldn't have a relationship with him. Too many obstacles stood in our way, not the least of which was that he thought I was my sister. But after that kiss at Kari's, I couldn't immediately break things off with him. That would make Kari look like some sort of trampy tease. And besides, I wanted to see Grant again. I craved it.

So I would allow myself to go on a date or two and then tell him it wasn't working out between us. Sometimes that's how things went. He probably wouldn't mind. The guy who'd never been turned down wouldn't have a hard time finding the next trophy girlfriend to take my place. I just had to make sure I didn't let my feelings get involved. I had to keep myself aloof.

Grant told me to dress casually and wear tennis shoes for our date, but I had no idea what he was planning. I also had no idea what I'd tell Maren about my absence or how I could go out without an entourage coming with me. It became a sort of mental game—thinking of different ways to escape.

After we flew back to California, Maren and I stopped by Kari's house. The art director had e-mailed mock-up covers for her new CD, and Maren wanted to get Kari's opinion on them.

Kari answered the door with a splint across her nose and bruises around her eyes. I gaped at her, wondering who had beat her up. Maren nearly dropped the covers. "What happened to you? Are you okay?" she asked.

"Did you call the police?" I asked at nearly the same time.

"Oh, this—" Kari touched her nose gingerly. "I got my dose done like Alegia's."

We both stared at her. "You what?" I asked.

"Once the swellig goes dowd, it will loog great. Everyone is goig to love it."

"Yeah, I already love it," I said, trying not to sound too horrified, "because it's *my* nose."

"Right. It looged good on you so I dew it would coordidate with the rest of my face."

I wanted to say, "You can't just copy my nose without my permission," which of course was stupid. She already had, and we were trying to look alike, but still. My nose was one of the few things that was mine, not hers.

Maren gritted her teeth. "You were supposed to be working on your songs. You're supposed to be recording them.

We've already announced you're debuting two new songs in San Diego. The show's less than a month away."

"I ca't regord lige this," Kari said. "I'm recoverig from surgery. I'm swolled, bruised, and my voice sounds lige it's fleeing through my dasal passage."

Maren let out an angry grunt, but she didn't yell. She just said, "We'll talk about your schedule tomorrow," and we left.

· · ·

Kari's surgery turned out to be a boon for me in a lot of ways.

The next morning, instead of planning out my schedule, Maren decided she needed to spend the day with Kari. As she gathered up her laptop and briefcase, I told her, "I'm going shopping later. I might be gone a while."

"Take Nikolay and Bao-Zhi, and only go to approved stores," she said and swept past me out the door without another word.

Escaping my entourage had just gotten a lot easier.

I wasn't about to take Nikolay out on a date with Grant, but since I'd been able to buy Bao-Zhi's silence with good tips, I had him chauffeur me to meet Grant. Our designated spot was a back road in the middle of nowhere. I felt sort of like an underworld spy, going to these lengths to avoid detection, but I didn't want to let anyone else take a picture of us together.

When we got there, I handed Bao-Zhi a wad of bills, told him I'd call when I needed him again, and climbed into Grant's Jaguar.

I should have been used to his good looks, to his square jaw and the sweep of his hair, but he looked at me and I lost the ability to speak. All I could do was mumble, "Hi."

Grant pulled onto the road. "Are you glad to be back home?"

Maren's house could never feel like home. "Yeah," I said.

Grant let his eyes drift from the road to my face. "I missed you."

The phrase struck a blow to my plan of aloofness, but I tried to hold firm. I shifted in my seat to put more distance between us. He didn't notice. He was back to watching the road. I tried to keep my voice businesslike. "So where are we going for this mystery date?"

"It's still a mystery," he said. "You won't know until we get there."

"Am I dressed right?"

His gaze ran over me, lingering on my face. "You look great."

It wasn't what I'd asked, but I still liked hearing it.

We made small talk, then finally pulled up to the airport. "What are we doing here?" I asked.

He didn't answer, just steered the car away from the terminals. We drove onto the tarmac and pulled up to a private jet.

I stared at it in disbelief. I should have known this wouldn't be like dating the guys in Morgantown.

As we got out of the car, I laughed nervously. A sudden fear sprung to my mind: Maybe he'd found out who I was and was sending me back to West Virginia. Instead he took my hand and stepped onto the plane with me. It looked almost identical to the one I'd come to California on, right down to the beige leather seats.

I sat down and buckled up, glad that I'd already been on a plane once so I knew how to work the safety belts. "So where are we going for our date that requires a plane?"

"You'll know when we get there," he said.

"I think that's something you say when you're kidnapping a person, not dating her."

He laughed, but didn't tell me. For the next hour we talked and ate a lunch of raspberry-glazed roast duckling and artichoke hearts. We might as well have been in some elite restaurant. And no matter how many different ways I asked, he still wouldn't tell me where the plane was headed.

When we landed, he took out a blindfold and slipped it over my eyes. "Have any more guesses as to where I'm taking you?"

"Right now I'm thinking a firing squad."

"Wrong again." He took my hand and led me slowly toward the exit door. As I stepped outside, a wall of heat engulfed me.

"Do you know where we are?" he asked.

"An oven? Hades?"

"Las Vegas," he said.

"Why are we in Las Vegas?" I reached for my blindfold, but he wouldn't let me take it off. He led me along the runway and then helped me step up into another vehicle. He climbed in beside me, buckled my safety belt, then put headphones over my ears. "You're going to need these in a minute," he said.

Before I could ask why, the vehicle shuddered and thumped with a loud chopping noise. I reached for my blindfold again, but Grant took hold of my hand. "Not yet," he called over the noise.

"Where are we?" I asked.

"Helicopter." He didn't let go of my hand. I interlaced my fingers with his and tried to figure out where we could be going. What was around Las Vegas that you couldn't drive to?

Wherever it was, it took an annoyingly long time to get there. But finally Grant reached around to the back of my hair and loosened the blindfold. I blinked in the light, adjusting my eyes, and the Grand Canyon came into focus in front of me.

I'd seen pictures of it before. And I knew the word *grand* meant big, yet I'd never imagined it could be so huge. I felt like a speck in a plunging rock sea. The world had suddenly become layered stacks of orange and brown.

I gasped and leaned closer to the window. "It's amazing."

"Better than pizza and a DVD?"

I squeezed his hand, but kept my gaze out the window. The helicopter made a lazy descent so that the canyon walls seemed to reach up and surround us. "You know, you've set a really bad precedent for first dates," I said. "How is anyone ever going to top this?"

I turned to him for the first time. He was watching me, not the scenery. "I brought you here because I wanted to see the look on your face when you saw this place." He smiled, and my heart flipped over. "It was worth the trip."

Eventually, the helicopter landed in a remote spot. We wouldn't have to worry about being seen down here. The pilot handed us a couple of backpacks with water, sunscreen, and hats. Then we stepped out into the vast landscape of towering rock walls. The Colorado River stretched out before us.

I knew long before Grant took hold of my hand again that my plan to remain emotionally uninvolved had disappeared somewhere among the layers of sun-baked stone.

• • •

The nice thing about Kari having surgery when she was supposed to be working was that Maren felt compelled to spend nearly every day of the next two weeks with her, "helping her concentrate on her music." It must not have been an easy task. Whenever she came back at night, it took her a while to unclamp her jaws. Even when she was home, she was always busy talking to Kari's agent, publicist, bodyguard, or choreographer. If I walked by Maren's office, I heard snippets about photo shoots, interviews, or concert paraphernalia. Since I didn't have any looming road trips, she hardly paid any attention to me.

Also, because Kari still had bruising and swelling from her nose job, she stayed out of the public eye, which meant I didn't have to worry about inadvertently creating multiple Kari sightings.

On most days after I finished my homework, workout, and dancing lessons, I'd tell Maren I was going shopping. Then I'd have Bao-Zhi drop me off at Rodeo Drive, and Grant would pick me up so we could do something together. Bao-Zhi was making a killing in tips.

A few times I took Nikolay along and actually went shopping. I bought some Prada jeans and designer tops. I had to in order for Maren not to get suspicious. Besides, they fit me perfectly, and a girl has to look her best for someone like Grant Delray.

But most of my shopping time actually consisted of eating at ultra-private restaurants with Grant or hanging out at his house in Malibu. Like Kari, he had a fence and a gate around his house to keep the press at a distance. So we could swim at his pool or even play basketball in his driveway. He always let me cheat at basketball, and I usually still lost. I didn't mind. For me, the point of the game was to watch his biceps in action.

Once we put on hats and sunglasses and went hiking in Topanga Canyon. It felt dangerous and just a little bit wicked to be out in the open where a passing hiker might recognize us. Things I wouldn't have thought twice about in West Virginia had suddenly become risky.

I made excuses to keep him away from Kari's place. "The paparazzi have been watching my house like crazy," I told him.

I knew I couldn't make this last. Every time we were together, I wanted to tell him the truth but was afraid it would be over between us as soon as he found out who I really was.

Kissing him was addictive. I had never fallen for a guy so quickly or so deeply. The term "falling in love" made perfect sense now. It did feel like free-falling—fast and thrilling, but leaving nothing to hang on to, no way to stabilize myself. Everything was beyond my control.

I couldn't even persuade myself to be logical and say, Hey, maybe there's another guy out there somewhere I'd like even better. This was Grant Delray. Handsome, talented, rich—hundreds of thousands of girls worshiped him, and they didn't even know the rest—that he was also down-to-earth and smart and could make people laugh anytime he wanted.

Besides, everything would change in a few weeks when I met my father. I would wait to see what happened there, then decide how to break the news to Grant.

CHAPTER 13

During the last week of April, I went out on another five-day tour of short concerts. Maren had underestimated how many jobs I'd be able to do for Kari when she first offered me the job. Kari's popularity was on the rise, and everyone wanted her at their events. At that point, I had a staggering $68,000 in my bank account. Kari's casino debts would have been nearly paid off with the revenue I'd brought in, except that Maren had to use a lot of the earnings to pay off credit cards and back taxes.

I offered to buy my mom a new car, but she refused to take my money. Which was perhaps why I couldn't bring myself to spend much of it. For all my angst over being poor, now that I had money, the only things I wanted to buy were things for her.

When I flew back into LA, things got more complicated. I had known that since Kari's face had healed she'd be out in the public again, but still I hadn't expected to see her on the front of *Us Weekly* holding hands with Michael. The caption read: *Back together again!*

Grant put a copy of the magazine in my lap when he picked me up from one of my shopping trips, then looked at me with raised eyebrows.

I stared into his ruggedly handsome face. I could have

told him everything. I should have. Instead I shrugged and said, "Must be an old picture."

And he believed me. Just like that, the subject dropped—I hoped for good. After all, Kari and Michael dating again wasn't that interesting of a story. It had already happened enough times. Besides, the paparazzi couldn't take many new pictures of Kari with Michael. Not while she was tucked out of sight working on her album and practicing for her mega concert.

Two days later, when I went over to Grant's house, he handed me a copy of the *National Enquirer*. I looked at the sidebar caption that read *Kari and Michael are reunited!* and my mouth went dry.

I managed a shrug as I handed it back to him. "I beat out reality shows and alien abductions for the cover. Cool."

He didn't smile. Instead he tilted his chin down. "How come the press keeps reporting that you're back with Michael?"

I forced a smile. "Well, the *National Enquirer* isn't known for its accuracy. Which reminds me—how are your plans of world domination coming along?"

I tried to slide into a hug and kiss him, but he put his hands on my shoulders and kept me at arm's length. His blue eyes clouded with suspicion. "You're not seeing both of us, are you?"

"No," I said, but his eyes still had an edge to them.

It suddenly became hard to look at him. I stared at the lettering on his T-shirt, at his neck, at the curve of his shoulder. And even then I could feel the weight of his gaze pressing against my heart.

So this was it. I had to tell him the truth now.

I let my arms drop away from him, then folded them across my chest so they didn't shake. "Here's the thing. I'm sorry I didn't tell you this before, but I'm not who you think I am. I'm not Kari Kingsley. I'm actually her . . . um . . ." How could I put this? "I'm her half sister from West Virginia that nobody knows about."

He rolled his eyes. "Very funny."

"No, really. She's seeing Michael, and I'm seeing you, and we just happen to look identical. Well, it's not completely coincidence—she had a nose job to look more like me."

"Okay, okay. You made your point. I'll believe you the first time." He leaned in and kissed me, and I considered what to do next. Telling him the truth had not gone how I expected. Although standing in his arms and kissing him was much better than the reaction I had anticipated.

Finally he stepped away from me, but he kept hold of my hand while we walked into his living room. His house wasn't nearly as big or as ostentatious as Kari's, and he'd barely decorated it. The living room mostly consisted of a couch, big-screen TV, and a black baby grand piano.

We sat down on his couch, still holding hands. I hoped the subject had passed. I just needed to ride it out for another two weeks until my father's concert, then I'd tell Grant everything.

Grant put his arm around my shoulder and lazily ran his

fingers through the ends of my hair. "We should think about going public with our relationship."

"Why?"

"Because then my band won't think I'm making up stuff about dating you, and I won't have family members dropping by and giving me magazines to keep me updated on my girlfriend's love life."

The sound of the word *girlfriend* on his lips stunned me for several seconds, and I just gazed at him.

"I know we won't have a minute of peace when the paparazzi find out we're a couple," he said, "but they're going to know about it sooner or later."

"Let's have it be later."

He kept running his fingers through my hair. "It would be good publicity for your next album. You and I splashed on magazine covers in every grocery store and newsstand in America."

My breath caught in my throat. If the paparazzi found out that I—that Kari—was seeing Grant when she was supposed to be dating Michael, my face really *could* be plastered on magazine covers around the country. And if that happened, would people who knew Kari be able to tell I was an imposter? Would people in my hometown recognize me?

Grant leaned away from me, a sudden smile on his lips. "I hadn't planned on giving this to you now, but I think I will." He stood up, walked over to the piano, and came back with a few sheets of music paper. "I was going to wait until

I had it finished. I still need to work on a few rough spots, but you'll get the main idea."

He handed me the sheets. It was a song he'd composed entitled "Give First Impressions a Second Chance."

The notes he'd penciled onto the paper meant nothing to me—I couldn't sight-read—but I could tell the lyrics were divided into parts. He'd written a duet for us to sing. The complete panic I felt was counterbalanced by the nice things he said. The refrain repeated in the chorus said: *If I'd believed that stuff was true, I would have missed out on loving you.*

He loved me? Was that just catchy lyrics, or did he mean it?

"Do you like it?" he asked.

"I love it."

A smile broke across his face, lighting up his features. "I was hoping you'd say that. Let's practice it right now."

He took my hand, trying to pull me toward the piano, but I stayed firmly seated on the couch. "Not right now." The second I sang anything to him, he'd realize I didn't have Kari's voice. I racked my brain to come up with a good excuse to turn him down. "I never mix business with pleasure, or work with dating, or singing with sitting with my boyfriend on the couch."

Boyfriend. I liked how that felt to say, and he didn't flinch when I said it. Boyfriend. Grant Delray was my boyfriend. I wanted to say it twelve more times just to taste the words in my mouth.

"I don't have the same policy," he said, and without taking his gaze off my eyes, he sang the first verse of our song. If there were any rough spots, like he'd claimed, I couldn't tell. I only heard his hypnotically beautiful voice surrounding me. At that moment I wanted nothing more in the world than to sing with him.

I would find a way to make our duet work somehow— some excuse, some explanation for the change in my voice. He leaned over and his lips found mine, and neither of us said anything for several minutes.

· · ·

While he drove me back to Rodeo Drive, Grant told me he would e-mail me a version of our song so I could practice it. I didn't say anything. My wishful thinking had begun to break apart. No matter how much I wanted it, I wouldn't be able to sing that song with him. But how long could I put him off about it?

"I guess I should warn you that my mom wants to invite you to dinner," he said. "She's been cooking vegetarian recipes to come up with something you'll like."

"Really?" I asked. I didn't want to meet his family. It was bad enough lying to Grant about my identity, I didn't want to spread the lie around to the rest of his family. "Don't you think it's a little early for that?"

He shrugged. "You've already met my dad, and I've met yours."

"What?" I asked. "When did you meet my father?"

Grant sent me a glance like he thought I should know. "I belonged to that group he put together to visit the troops last year."

"Oh, right," I said. The words sounded harshly hollow, even to me. I didn't know why they'd come out that way.

"He's a nice guy," Grant said. "You remind me of him sometimes—your sense of humor and your mannerisms."

There is obviously something wrong with me. A normal person would not cry after hearing that. And I'm not even sure why I started crying—whether it was the unfairness that Grant knew my father better than I did or because it was the first time anyone had ever said I reminded him of my father. Could I really have his sense of humor? Was that inherited?

I couldn't help thinking, with more desperation than I wanted to admit, that if I was like him, if my father could see himself in me, maybe he'd love me.

Grant looked over and then did a double take. "What?" he asked in alarm. "What's wrong?"

I shook my head. "Nothing." But I knew he wouldn't be satisfied with that answer, so I added, "It's just things with my father aren't the way I want them to be right now."

Grant's voice went soft. "You can change that if you want."

"It's not that simple."

"Why don't you pick up the phone and call him?"

I didn't have his phone number, for one thing.

I wondered—just to inflict pain on myself—if Grant had his phone number. How many friends, acquaintances, and near strangers talked to him every day? But even if Grant had Alex Kingsley's number, I couldn't ask him for it. How do you explain to a guy that you don't know your own father's phone number without raising major red flags?

I wiped the tears off of my cheeks, angry with myself for having these emotional reactions every time I learned something about my father. He hadn't spent one ounce of emotion thinking about me.

"I know you two don't get along anymore," Grant said. "That's in chapter nine of Lorna's book, but I'm sure he wants to talk to you as badly as you want to talk to him."

Probably not.

I slipped on a pair of sunglasses and grabbed my hat from off of the seat. We'd arrived at Rodeo Drive, and he was about to let me off. As Grant put the car in park, I reached over and squeezed his hand. "Thanks for trying to help. And the song is beautiful. It means a lot to me."

He leaned over and kissed me. It was stupid to let him do it in public, but I didn't turn away. Being within six inches of him apparently disarmed my rational thought. Besides, it only lasted three seconds. What were the chances that anyone would have a camera pointed at us during those three seconds?

• • •

The next day Grant e-mailed me an updated version of our song. He not only sent the sheet music, he also sent a video of him singing his part so I could practice.

Maren wasn't around. She'd gone to the studio to keep an eye on Kari. So I sat in the living room practicing the duet until I had the words memorized. I tried to sound like Kari. I tried to copy her strong, rich voice. The good news: I sounded pretty good, light and lyrical. The bad news: It didn't matter how many times I repeated it, I didn't sound like Kari. I still sounded like me.

What was I going to do next time I saw him? He'd want to practice it. I would have to fake some horrible sore throat, and how long would he buy that?

It's funny how sometimes you worry about things turning out badly, but you don't even consider that they could actually end up much worse.

The next day, while I was doing homework, Maren came home from one of her outings with Kari. Without speaking, she dropped two tabloids on the table next to me.

On the front page of one, I walked out of the restaurant by Grant's side; in the other, I kissed Grant in his car. The headlines of the first read "Kari and Grant's Secret Weekend Getaway!" The second said "Kari Cheats on Michael!"

As I stared at them, Maren's words dropped down to me like falling ice chunks. "Kari's friends have called her about these. Michael has seen them too. You can imagine the day I've had."

"I'm sorry—"

She flung one hand out in my direction. "Oh, I did a great job of transforming you into Kari. Even Kari's boyfriend thought it was her."

My stomach clenched. "Is he really upset?"

"We'll know how mad he is just as soon as he starts speaking to her again."

"I didn't mean—"

She put her hands on the table, leaned toward me, and yelled, "I don't care what you meant! What did you think you were doing, sneaking around with Grant Delray?"

I couldn't answer her. It didn't matter; she didn't wait for my reply. "You will call him right now and break up with him. Then you're never to go near him again. Do you understand?"

I didn't move. Grant's face looked up at me from the tabloid article, Grant's perfectly chiseled face next to mine. Maren walked over to the coat closet where I kept my purse and yanked my cell phone out of it. She thrust it into my hand. "Do it now, or so help me, I'll call him as your assistant and break up with him for you. And I won't be nice about it."

"No," I said, "you're not going to do that."

Her eyes hardened as though I'd offered a challenge and she opened my cell phone. "Watch me."

I sat up straighter, holding my ground. "If you call him, I'll quit this job. How much money does Kari still owe to casinos and credit cards?"

Her fingers paused on the buttons as she considered my words.

"I know what matters to you," I said. "You didn't arrange events to help Kari. You want to pay off Kari's debts so Alex Kingsley will be impressed with what a wonderful mother you'd be for her."

Maren slid the phone shut, but her expression seemed far from defeated. She dug through her purse, a sudden calmness about her. "You're right. You do know what I care about, but I know what you care about too." She pulled two pieces of paper from her purse and held them up: an Alex Kingsley concert ticket and a backstage pass. "I'm just not sure *why* you care."

She lowered her chin, waiting for my answer. When I remained silent, she let out a scoffing grunt. "He's old enough to be your father, you know."

"Yes, actually, I'm aware of that."

She tapped the ticket against the palm of her hand, watching me, calculating. Her lips turned up ever so slightly, more of a sneer than a smile. "Why throw away your job over Grant? He doesn't care about you anyway. You know that, don't you, Alexia? That Grant Delray doesn't care about some little nobody from West Virginia. He likes Kari Kingsley. And no matter how much you look like her, you'll never be her. So it can't work out between you."

I didn't answer. I churned with anger, but I couldn't argue with her. I'd thought the same things myself. I'd thought them and tried to dismiss them, but I was afraid they were true.

"We'll make a deal." Maren handed me my phone, then held the ticket and pass out to me. "You break up with Grant and you can have these. Otherwise the job is over and I'll tell Alex's staff to be on the watch for a Kari Kingsley impersonator—one who's a stalker and has delusions of actually being Kari. You'll never get past security to meet him."

I stood up, mentally revising my opinion of Kari's lamp-throwing as a solution for dealing with problems. Chucking one of Maren's lamps across the room seemed like a great idea. I didn't do it, though. I guess I'd controlled my behavior as Kari for so long that controlling my behavior as Alexia didn't seem much harder.

Maren folded her arms, tucking the ticket and pass out of sight. "And don't even think about making trouble for me. Remember, I have sales receipts where you wrote Kari's name to buy clothes. Granted, it was part of our little game, but the law doesn't know that. If I reported that someone had taken one of Kari's cards, the police would consider your signature forgery and identity theft." She took slow steps around me, circling the way vultures did. "I imagine Grant wouldn't be impressed if you got hauled off to prison. And of course, Alex would really look down on someone with a criminal record. He's funny that way. Was that how you wanted to meet him? Maybe he could come down to the police station to confirm that you're not really his daughter."

With every sentence she spoke, I felt the blood drain from my face. Never once had I thought she would resort to blackmail. Now I realized I'd put myself at risk for that all along. Maren had given me a credit card in Kari's name so I could sign for things while I pretended to be her. Of course it would seem to everyone like I'd stolen from Kari.

I felt a sick thud in my stomach. That's what my father's first impression of me would be—that I'd taken advantage of my resemblance to Kari in order to tap into one of her bank accounts.

"I have a copy of my job contract," I said. "Maybe the police would like to see that."

Maren flicked one hand as though shooing a fly. No concern, no glimmer of worry leaked from her eyes. "I'll say it's forged. Trust me, the police would believe Kari Kingsley's manager and not the teenage girl who's used Kari's credit card." She shook her head, and this time the smile was real, almost sympathetic. "I should point out that your staff will be loyal to me. One thing you need to learn is that I always cover myself."

I clenched my hands together, feeling trapped. What proof did I have that everything I'd done had been under Maren's direction? I desperately tried to think of anything I could offer to the authorities on my behalf.

Maren took a step closer. "It doesn't have to come to that, of course. I really hope it doesn't. As of now, you still have a very lucrative job." She held the ticket and the pass back out to me. "So which will you choose: Grant Delray, whom you can't have anyway, or this job and a meeting with Alex Kingsley?"

At that moment, I looked at my life, a bystander for the first time, observing everything I'd done since I found out that Alex Kingsley was my father.

When I'd stormed away from my mom at the hotel, I'd told her I wanted to find out who I was. I'd found out. I was the type of girl who could be talked into doing things if the price was right, the type of girl who deceived thousands of people who'd paid to see a rock star sing. Worse yet, I'd lied to the guy I loved.

This was the girl I wanted to introduce to my father?

How had I become so false in such a short time?

I walked to Maren and took the ticket and pass. "You're right. It's time I have a talk with Grant. I'll do it in person." I turned the ticket and the pass over in my hand, then ripped them in two. I handed the pieces back to Maren. "You can consider this my resignation."

I turned and walked away from her, grabbing my purse as I went to the front door. I expected her to call out to me, to say either "If you're done working for me, then don't come back here—you can go directly to the airport," or maybe "Don't be so rash, Alexia—you can still make a lot of money." But whatever she thought, she didn't say it.

Outside the sky was blue, the landscaping vibrant, and my stomach so knotted I felt like I could easily throw up. I used my cell phone to call a cab and told the driver he'd find me walking down Montana Avenue. I didn't know who I would go see first, Grant or Kari. Grant would be harder to face; Kari would be more complicated to talk to, especially since she was mad at me over the tabloids.

I should see Kari first. She was my sister. I owed her an explanation or at least an apology.

But my mind wouldn't let go of Grant and the words Maren had said. *Grant Delray doesn't care about some little nobody from West Virginia. He likes Kari Kingsley. And no matter how much you look like her, you'll never be her.*

I trudged down the street, feeling sicker with every footstep, then I called the one person who would understand how I felt: my mother. It was nearly eight P.M. in West Virginia. I tried to imagine what she was doing.

She picked up after a few rings. "Hello?"

"Mom, it's Lexi. I want you to do something for me. Can you go to the bookcase in my bedroom?"

"Okay, just a second." I heard her walk through the house. "All right, I'm here."

"Next to my journal there's a magazine. I want you to pull it out and look at the guy on the cover."

I heard her shuffling through books, then she let out a low breath. "Oh, *qué guapo.*"

"Yeah, he's gorgeous. We've been dating for a few weeks, and I'm totally in love with him."

Mom's voice rose with worry. "What do you mean when you say totally in love?"

"Totally, stupidly, can't think about anything else. But here's the thing: He thinks I'm Kari." And then my voice cracked. It felt like I was reliving my mother's life. "He only likes me because I look like someone else."

"That's the only reason he likes you, because of how you look?"

"Well, no, but he thinks I'm Kari—a famous rock star. I can't keep him from finding out the truth, though. The tabloids spotted us together and now they're saying Kari is cheating on her boyfriend, and Kari isn't going to let that slide. Which reminds me, you might want to keep Abuela out of the grocery store for a while. I'm sort of on the cover of the *National Enquirer* kissing Grant."

She sputtered. "You're what?"

I didn't have time to go into an explanation of that. "Mom, I don't know what to do. I'm so afraid of losing him."

For a moment she didn't say anything. I wondered if she was thinking about how she'd felt about Alex Kingsley when she was my age. Then she said, "You need to tell him the truth. He needs to know who you really are."

I waited for her to say more. She didn't. I said, "Mom, that didn't work out very well for you. Alex Kingsley knew who you were and he never called you back. I've seen pictures of his Grammy dates, though. They were starlets, singers, and supermodels."

Her words grew painfully quiet. "I know. But if Grant doesn't like you for who you are, then he's not worth it."

It was true, and yet I still didn't feel that way. I wondered if she felt Alex Kingsley wasn't worth it. It seemed to me if she had, she would have burned those posters of him long ago.

"The longer you put it off, the more difficult it's going to be," she said.

My steps on the sidewalk faltered until I hardly moved. "I know." I hadn't expected her to tell me any different. She couldn't have offered up some magical solution. Still, I needed to know that at least one person understood how hard this was.

"I told Maren that I quit," I said. "I'll try to get a flight out tonight."

"You're leaving before you've met your father?"

For a moment I thought of staying and trying to meet him, but the desire had vanished. I couldn't imagine telling him what I'd done or pretending none of it had happened. "When I get home, I'll think about having a lawyer contact him. Then if he wants to meet me, he can come out to West Virginia."

"We'll talk about it when you get here," she said. I knew she meant to soothe me, but it only made my failure sting worse.

I hung up with my mom and then texted Grant, asking where he was. He texted back, "I'm done with a music video and about to go home. Where are you?"

"On my way to your house," I wrote. The cab picked me up ten minutes later, and I gave him Grant's address.

CHAPTER 14

The entire cab ride there, I tried to formulate how to tell Grant the truth. When the cab pulled up to his house, I still hadn't figured it out. I paid the driver extra and told him to wait for me. I hoped I wouldn't need a ride to Kari's quickly, but I figured it was better to be prepared.

Grant met me at the door with a hug, then shut the door behind me. I leaned into him, breathing in the scent of his cologne and imprinting it into my mind.

"I know what you want to talk about," he said. "You saw the tabloids from this morning, didn't you?"

"Maren showed them to me."

He put his hands on my shoulders and held me a little ways away, looking into my eyes. "Judging from your expression, you weren't too happy with the coverage."

"It complicates things."

His hands traveled down my shoulders to my hands, and he pulled me closer to him again. "I know. My publicist has been getting calls from shows and magazines wanting to know what our relationship is." He leaned closer, keeping his gaze on my eyes. "I figured I should talk to you before I announced anything." But then he didn't talk. He leaned down and kissed me. I wound my arms around his neck and kissed him back, trying to capture this moment, to clasp it, so I could always remember what it felt like to hold him this way. If I just kept kissing him, I would never have to let him go.

He lifted his head and rubbed his hand across my back. "So was that a 'they're a happy couple and don't have any further comment' sort of kiss?"

"No, that was a 'we need to talk more about it' sort of kiss."

He smiled and his eyes glinted. "If that's how we're going to talk about it, I'm happy to discuss it with you at length." He bent down and his lips brushed against mine again.

I stepped away from him. "No, I meant we should really talk about it."

"Okay." He took hold of my hand and pulled me into the living room. "That reminds me—did you go over the duet?"

"Yeah, it's a beautiful song, especially the part that says you should give people a second chance. . . ."

We'd reached the couch, and he sat down. I sat beside him, noticing all the little things I loved about him. His broad shoulders. The curve of his jaw. The rich brown color of his hair.

"I'm glad you like it," he said. "If we hurry and spend some time practicing it, we could debut it at your concert next Friday."

No, we couldn't. I ran my free hand through my hair,

suddenly hating it for being blond. I wanted it to be brunette again so at least something about me was real.

He tugged at my hand, mistaking my agitation for something else. "I know you've been working hard preparing for your concert and you're nervous about it, so I'm bringing you a surprise. I think you'll like it."

He'd never talked about coming to my concert before, but I should have known he would plan on it. Why had I let things go so far? How could I have let myself get into this situation? This had always been a disaster waiting to happen—I just hadn't seen it. Even if Maren hadn't threatened me, I would still have been here having the same conversation in not too many days.

He squeezed my hand. "Why do you look so serious?"

I raised my eyes to his, staring at their deep blue color. His eyes would be the easiest things about him to remember. "You really want to tell people we're a couple?"

He shrugged as though it was obvious. "Of course."

"Let me ask you a question. Would you still want everyone to know we were a couple if I wasn't a celebrity?"

I knew he'd say yes. Whether he actually meant it remained to be seen, but I was sure he would say yes.

Instead he let go of my hand and slid his arm around my shoulder. "Listen, I know you're concerned about your debts and Lorna's book, but you're too young to worry about being a has-been. Who knows, maybe the book could be a good thing. After it comes out, you can go on the talk shows, give your rebuttal, and then sing something from your new album. It'll be great publicity. And *People* will pay a ton of money to get the first scoop interview about how hurt you are that a former employee turned on you this way. Lorna might be doing you a favor."

Which wasn't my point. I tried again. "Okay, but I mean if I was a small-town girl, living in a . . . well . . . a small town, if I was just a normal person. Would you still be interested in me?"

His gaze ran over me, and a grin slid across his face. "You're too talented to be a normal person. Normal people don't have hit songs on the radio." As though to prove it, he stood and pulled me up with him. He towed me in front of a large mirror that hung in the entryway hall. "Look at yourself."

I did. I looked at my long blond hair and at him standing behind me, hands on my shoulders. I looked at the muscles in his arms and his perfect features.

He lowered his face to speak softly in my ear. "You surpassed normal a long time ago, and there's no going back to being one of the nameless masses. When our relationship goes public, I'm going to be the envy of every guy."

No, he wouldn't be.

He smiled at my reflection. "The tabloids will say I'm way outclassed, and I won't mind because they'll be right, and I'm glad for it."

His arms wrapped around me, and he tilted his head to kiss my neck. I watched our reflections in the mirror and felt numb. He'd answered my question. It just wasn't the answer I wanted. And despite my intentions, I couldn't tell him who I was. I couldn't face the rejection stoically the way my mother had. I didn't want to go back to West Virginia and cherish his picture on a magazine cover and wait for a phone call that never came.

Well, I would cherish his picture, but I would do it with my pride intact. One day he'd figure out the truth. He was bound to run into the real Kari sooner or later, but I'd be long gone by that time.

"I lied to you," I said.

He lifted his head, only mildly concerned until he saw my expression. Then his eyes grew sharp.

I swallowed hard. "I lied to you about a lot of things." The numbness inside chilled me—sent out frozen tendrils winding around my heart. I was shaking and couldn't stop. "I'm sorry."

He dropped his arms back to his sides. "You lied? About what—Michael?"

I forced myself to nod. "We're together, and the stuff in the tabloids about us was true. In fact, a lot of stuff in Lorna's book is true too. I'm not who you thought I was." I turned away from the mirror, away from him. I'd hurt him, and I couldn't stand to see the shock in his eyes.

I headed across the room. As I opened the front door, he took hold of my arm. "That's it? That's all you're going to say? I don't deserve an explanation?"

Before I had a chance to answer, he looked past me to the waiting taxi. At the sight of it, he let out punctured breath, and his gaze turned on me in accusation. "You told your taxi to wait. You only came here to break up, didn't you?" He let go of my arm as though I suddenly disgusted him. "Don't let me hold up your plans. I'm sure you have places to go."

I went out the door, pushing myself to go forward. Every move felt stiff, awkward. I heard my footsteps thud down his driveway. I thought vaguely, ridiculously, that Kari wouldn't have approved of my walk. Then I got to the taxi, opened the door, and sank inside.

I wasn't going to look back. There was no point in checking to see if the door had already shut, but I couldn't help myself. I turned around in my seat and saw Grant standing in his doorway, arms folded, eyes narrow, watching me leave.

. . .

I told the driver to take me to Kari's house and then to the airport. I didn't want to go back to Maren's to pick up my clothes or things. As long as I kept myself focused on what I had to do, I could get through this. I could even make it through this car ride like a normal passenger and not curl into the fetal position and sob uncontrollably in the back-seat.

I would say good-bye to Kari, apologize for the trouble I'd caused with Grant, and give her the sapphire necklace. I felt she should have it, since it was bought for her mother.

My hand went to the chain around my throat, fingering it as I looked outside at the passing cars. I'd worn it so many days that it felt like it belonged to me. But I couldn't keep it any more than I could keep anything else from Kari's life. None of it was mine. It was this thought that snapped my willpower. The tears I'd held in since Grant's house came out.

. . .

Once I reached Kari's I pulled myself together. I had to. Maren's car was parked in the driveway. If I had to see her again, I wouldn't do it crying. I sat in the back of the taxi for a few moments fanning my face with my hands as though this would make my eyes less red. Several deep breaths later, I emerged from the taxi and walked to Kari's door.

"How long do you want to me to wait for you this time?" the driver asked.

I didn't dare think about how big of a bill I was racking up in cab fare. "I won't be long," I said.

Even before I reached the door, I could hear their voices inside, yelling at each other.

My steps grew slower. Were they fighting about me? Was Kari angry that Maren had driven me to quit or was Kari just still yelling about the pictures of Grant and me in the tabloids? Maybe she blamed Maren for not keeping better tabs on my whereabouts.

I looked back at the taxi longingly, then knocked on the door. Whatever the fight was about, I would face it.

No one answered. They probably couldn't hear me. I tried the door, found it unlocked—of course—and pushed it open.

Kari was sitting on the floor in the entryway, surrounded by shopping bags. At least a dozen of them. There were shoe boxes and hat boxes and dresses in clear plastic. It looked like Christmas without a tree.

Maren held a tennis bracelet, shaking it at Kari. "How could you spend twenty thousand dollars on this when you already have another one like it?"

"I needed to make myself feel better!" Kari yelled back at her.

Both of them glanced my direction as I came in the door, but neither of them spoke to me.

Maren made a sweeping motion at the bags and boxes. "You're taking this back. Every single thing. In fact, I'll do it for you right now." She picked up one of the bags, but Kari reached out and held on to the other end.

"You will not!" Kari yelled. "That would be totally humiliating. The store clerks will think I can't afford it."

"You *can't* afford it!" Maren let go of the bag, but snatched up another. "You're still nearly a million in debt. Do you know how much money that is?" She yanked another bag off the floor. "There's not a thing in the world you don't already have, and you gave your word you wouldn't go shopping until you finished the album." She grabbed two more bags and didn't have room to hold more. She looked at the clutter on the floor, clearly unhappy to leave it with Kari. She kicked one bag with her foot and shouted, "Don't touch anything!" then turned and carried her armload of bags outside.

As soon as she'd gone out the door, Kari turned to me, lips in a tight line. "Do you know what it was like seeing myself kissing Grant Delray on the cover of the *Enquirer*? How could you do this, Alexia? You weren't supposed to see Grant again. I told you that."

"I know. I'm sorry."

"You're *so* fired!" She picked up two bags and stood up as though she didn't know what to do with them. She took a step, then glanced at me and stopped. She let out a whimper and sank back down on the floor. "Don't stare at me like that. I know I have a problem, okay? I know it."

She looked around at the boxes and bags still surrounding her as though seeing them for the first time. "It isn't my fault, though. I have to do something when I'm upset. And everyone saw those pictures in the tabloids." She reached into a bag and pulled out a cream leather miniskirt. She laid it across her lap, smoothing it out with the care of someone caressing a new baby blanket. "I looked so beautiful in the store when I tried this on. The owner herself picked it out, and the salesgirls said I should wear it in my next video. I can't take this back." She shrugged and her eyes teared up. "I can't take any of it back. People will talk, and they're already bad-mouthing me. They think I'm cheating on my boyfriend."

So this shopping binge was my fault. I stared at a pair of snakeskin pumps and wondered how much they cost. "I'm sorry about the pictures," I said. "I didn't mean for things to go that far." I walked to the wall where Kari sat and slid down beside her. "I was too in love with Grant to think about it clearly. But it's going to be okay now. I broke up with him."

Kari gave a half grunt. "No wonder you look so terrible." She took the miniskirt from her lap and put it on mine. "Here, you need this more than I do."

"Maren won't let either of us keep it."

"You don't think I can get around her?" Kari stood, went to one of the antique chests in the entryway, and put the skirt inside. She sat back down against the wall right before Maren came inside again. Without speaking to either one of us, Maren picked up two more bags and a couple of shoe boxes. She tucked them under her arms and headed back outside to her car.

Kari opened a box that sat at her side. She gingerly pulled apart a Styrofoam container and took out a shiny Siamese cat figurine no larger than her palm. "Do you like it?" She turned the cat over in her hands. "I always wanted a kitten when I was little, but I'm allergic, so my dad bought me the glass kind. I have over a hundred now."

I looked at the cat in her hand, and I swallowed hard. "He loves you, you know."

She shook her head and wouldn't stop shaking it. "He cut me off. Won't give me another cent. He doesn't like how

I spend my money, but the thing is, he's the reason I keep spending it." Her hand tightened on the cat. "I used to drink when I got upset—like Lorna wrote in her book. He made me promise I'd stop. So now I only gamble or go shopping when I'm upset, and why can't everybody be glad it's not worse than that?" She raised the cat above her head. "It's his fault for not caring, and your fault for those stupid pictures, and Maren's fault for letting me keep my credit cards when she knows I'm a compulsive shopper." At the last word, she threw the cat against the wall and it exploded into a hundred shards of glass.

"Well," she said with satisfaction. "I guess Maren won't be returning that."

I winced at the mess and couldn't help the words that popped out of my mouth. "How much did that cost?"

She picked up the box and threw it against the wall too. "Not much. Probably about ten minutes of your next event."

"I'm not doing any more appearances for you. I already told Maren that I quit, and besides, you just fired me."

She blinked, taken aback. "Well, now I'm unfiring you. Instead I want you to work overtime. You owe me that much."

I shook my head. "I came here to tell you good-bye." The words got hard to say. I had to push out the rest. "If you ever want to call or text something—I'd really like that."

Kari's voice raised an octave, her face flushed with panic. "You can't leave! I need you!"

I hadn't heard Maren come back inside, but she was there gathering up another armful of things. "That's another reason you need to cut back on your expenses, Kari. Alexia is tired of being you."

"You're tired of being me?" Kari repeated each word as though they'd come with a slap in the face.

"It's not that." I watched as Maren headed back out the door, and I lowered my voice. "I never should have done this in the first place. It ended up hurting people."

Kari put her hand on my arm. "But I forgive you about Grant. You don't have to leave because of that."

I was glad she forgave me and wished Grant's forgiveness could have been so easily obtained. "Thanks," I said. "But I need to go home. I have a present to give you before I leave, though." I pulled the chain upward, revealing the sapphire pendant. As I spoke, I ran my thumb over its surface, saying good-bye to it. "My dad gave this to my mom before he left her. It's the only thing he ever gave us. You know how you never knew your mom? Well, I never knew my dad. I know how that feels, to grow up missing a piece of you like that." I took the necklace off and held it out to her. "I want you to have this."

I had expected her to be touched, moved by the gesture. Instead her eyes looked at the necklace in horror. "I can't take that."

"I want you to. And when you wear it, you can remember you're not alone. You have so many people who love you—your fans, your father, me."

She shook her head and then crossed her arms as though to make sure I didn't put it in her hand. "Don't say you love me—you don't even care what happens. You're leaving when I need you more than ever. I'm not going out in public anymore. I'm not."

"Kari, you dance and sing better than I ever could. You can do everything I've done."

"I can't. I'm never going where the paparazzi can find me again." She put her head down on her knees and let out a moan. I had no idea what I'd said that had upset her, but then I heard Maren's voice. She'd come back inside and instead of picking up the remaining bags, she stood in the doorway with her hands on her hips. "Kari, did you say something to the press while you were out today?"

Kari moaned again.

"What did you say this time?"

Kari didn't answer.

Maren walked over to Kari, hands still on her hips. "Just tell me how bad it was."

Kari peered over her knees, hugging her legs. "I tried to avoid them. I wore sunglasses and a hat. Someone at Gucci must have tipped them off. When I came out of the store, a cameraman was waiting. He asked if I was dating both Michael and Grant."

Maren put her hand on her temple. "What did you say?"

"Not at the same time."

Maren groaned and shut her eyes.

Kari held a hand out in her defense. "What could I say? Everyone has seen those pictures of me kissing Grant."

Maren looked at the ceiling and sighed. "You couldn't have thought of something that wasn't quite so incriminating?"

"I don't think well when cameras are in my face." Kari put her head back on her knees. "So I'm not going out in public again. Ever."

Maren let her gaze fall back onto Kari. "You have the concert in San Diego in exactly one week."

"And I'm not doing it."

"You have to. You need the money. You'll lose your house if you miss more payments."

Kari lifted her head enough to look at me. "Alexia can do it."

I shook my head. "No, I can't."

She blinked, and new tears ran down her cheeks. "My boyfriend thinks I'm sneaking around with Grant Delray. And I can't blame him, since the rest of the world thinks it too. They all hate me. If you'd kept away from Grant like you were supposed to, none of this would have happened. And now you're leaving me. Thanks a million. It's about what I'm short."

I stared at her openmouthed. I did feel awful about what I'd done, but I didn't want to stay another minute. Besides, it was one thing to lip-synch a few songs at a rodeo or places like that; it was another thing to do a real concert. Those were major productions. Despite Jacqueline's training, I didn't have the skill to pull it off.

"I can't do that many dance routines, and besides, your backup dancers won't be fooled by me. They'll know I'm an imposter."

Kari nodded as though making a mental list. "We'll have to get new backup dancers."

I turned to Maren, waiting for her to step in and point out the impossibility of me performing a full-blown concert in a week. Instead her gaze grew calculating. She looked first at me and then at Kari. "I'll help Alexia pull it off on one condition."

"What?" I asked—although I meant *What are you talking about?* and not *What is your one condition?*

Maren ignored me. "Kari, you have to enter some sort of treatment program."

Kari let her knees drop down to the floor. "You think I need to go to rehab?"

"You need help dealing with your problems in a healthy way."

Kari folded her arms and looked away from us. "I don't. No."

Maren picked up the last of the bags, but instead of holding it, she dropped it into Kari's lap. "Fine, then, Alexia goes home, I quit, and you can figure out how to pay your bills on your own."

Kari grabbed hold of the bag, until the paper crackled in

protest. "The press will eat me alive if I'm in rehab. I'll lose the rest of my product endorsements."

"They won't know," Maren said, "because Alexia will put on your concert."

"Wait a minute—" I said, but neither of them listened.

Kari let out a groan. "All right. You win. I'll go to rehab."

"Good. After I check you in, I'll see to it that Alexia is ready." Maren eyed me as though I were a dress that needed serious alterations.

"I never said I would do this," I protested.

Maren raised one eyebrow at me coolly. "You're saying this after you just told Kari how much you cared about her? If you meant it, you'd want her to get help."

I looked at Kari, at her eyes that were puffy from crying. She'd not only lost her boyfriend, she was going to have to endure more public mocking, and it was my fault. How could I not agree? I lifted my hands, then let them drop. "Okay, I'll do the concert, but when it's over I'm going home." I stood up, so frustrated I wanted to kick something. I should have left when I could have. I should have mailed the stupid necklace to her. "The taxi driver is still waiting. I'd better tell him he can leave."

Maren smiled. "I already did."

Which meant she had known all along I would be staying. I glared at her, but she turned away from me, picked up the last of Kari's purchases, and went back to her car.

For the next six days, I did nothing but work on my dance routines. All sorts of new moves were added for the concert. For the first number I came up onstage through an elevator in the floor while flares went off. I performed one song on a swing—sometimes standing on it, sometimes sitting and swinging, sometimes twirling around until I couldn't see straight. By the end of the second day of practice, I'd heard Kari's songs played so relentlessly that I hated every single one.

I worked with a set of backup dancers that Maren had hired just for the concert. They picked up the routines effortlessly while I struggled and forgot what moves came next. And they had even harder parts than I did.

The entertainment shows gave Kari's botched dating explanation a lot of play time. The late-night shows commented on it too. They said things like "Well, who would have thought? It looks like Kari Kingsley is a natural blonde, after all."

I winced every time someone said something about her. I couldn't forget that the pictures with Grant were my fault. I was just glad Kari wasn't allowed to watch TV in the treatment center. She was off in the Utah mountains somewhere, getting in touch with her core values and working on her inner strength. Her album's release date was pushed back again.

She called me a couple of times during the week to see

how things were going. I practically begged her to come back and do the concert every time I talked to her, which is perhaps why she didn't call more often. And despite the fact that she was working on her lack of inner strength, she always found enough inner strength to turn me down. "I need to be here," she said. "I'm learning all sorts of stuff about myself."

And I learned all sorts of stuff about myself too. Like the fact that I could barely walk after doing leg kicks for half the day.

Grant texted me after Kari's impromptu street interview first came out. He wrote, "I'm not surprised that you lied about us. I just can't figure out why you play dumb in front of the camera. What's with that?"

I didn't know how to reply. I must have stared at my phone for ten minutes. I wanted to call him. I wanted to hear his voice. A part of me still wished that somehow I could make things work out between us. I couldn't call, though. He would ask too many questions I couldn't answer. I texted back, "I'm sorry."

On the day of the concert, I was so nervous I could hardly eat. For once Maren had to force me to put food in my mouth. She said I'd need all the energy I could get.

I practiced in the morning at the concert hall and we ran through everything. The tech people kept adjusting the lights, the sound, and special effects, but the dance routines went okay. I made a few mistakes. I wasn't used to the huge spotlights or firework fountains shooting off around me.

I had a short rest at the hotel, then went back to the concert hall for hair and makeup. My costume consisted of a black-and-gold leotard and a gold-sequined miniskirt. I looked like Las Vegas's version of a tiger showgirl.

Maren, I admit, was in her element. She kept everyone away from me, including reporters and radio show personalities who wanted to talk about my relationship with Grant and Michael. Officially, Kari didn't have a comment. Thankfully, neither did Grant or Michael.

I knew through Maren that Michael had broken up with Kari and told her that when she'd worked out her commitment issues she could give him a call. She couldn't call and tell him she wanted him and only him until after the concert, though. Otherwise he'd show up and find me.

Which meant Kari wanted this concert to be over nearly as much as I did.

The opening act went on, and I was left in the green room, where I compulsively went over every dance number in my mind. I felt shaky, but at the same time so full of adrenaline I couldn't sit in one place. I checked my reflection in the mirror. Everything looked fine, glittery, but fine. I took deep measured breaths. That was supposed to calm people down. Or maybe it was just supposed to help in childbirth, I couldn't remember anymore.

A knock came at the door. I hoped it was just someone asking if I needed a bottled water and not Maren giving me more instructions I probably wouldn't retain.

As I opened the door, the first person I saw was Grant.

He stood with hands thrust into his jacket pockets. His blue eyes seemed cold and formal, but besides that, he looked every bit as handsome as the last time I'd seen him. A sharp pang of longing twisted into my heart. I stared at him, desperately searching for words that would tell him how I felt. "Grant," was all I could come up with.

"No matter how things ended between us," he said, "I told you I had a surprise for you, and I still thought I should give it to you." He stepped aside and for the first time, I noticed someone stood behind him. My father, Alex Kingsley, walked into the room.

CHAPTER 15

Grant turned and strode down the hallway without saying good-bye. Any other time, I would have gone after him. I would have apologized again—something, but I could barely stand, let alone run after him. The air had gone out of my lungs. I stared at my father without blinking.

He was taller than I'd imagined, and looked older—in my mind's eye I'd kept seeing him on the cover of the CDs we'd had since I was a child. Each wrinkle around his eyes and the gray hair at his temples surprised me. He was fit, though, and had a confident energy.

I was torn between wanting to throw my arms around him and wanting to turn and run away. Instead I stood before him silent and trembling.

He looked me over from head to toe, his thumbs casually looped through his jeans pockets. His voice was calm, but the edge to his voice showed that he wasn't amused. "So who are you, and where is my daughter?"

"Kari has been in rehab for the last week." My words came out more composed than I felt. I was finally meeting my father, and I was wearing a sequined gold miniskirt. "Maren didn't want people to know about Kari's problems, so she hired me to double for her."

"Rehab?" he repeated.

"For compulsive shopping, mostly."

He relaxed a little when I said that, like he'd been afraid it was something worse, but accusation still colored his tone. "Maren told me that Kari was doing better, that she was out doing events to pay off her debts."

"That was me too," I said. "Kari was working on her album."

"The album that's not done."

I prickled on her behalf. "She wanted to come up with hit songs on her own, so you would be proud of her." This wasn't exactly what Kari had said. She had said she wanted to come up with hit songs to prove to him that she could do it, and maybe I was transferring my own motivations to Kari—but I didn't think so. She had a whole roomful of ceramic cats because he had given her some as a child. She wanted his approval.

His gaze went to the door, and his voice came out terse. "Well, I'm real proud right now." Then he turned and left the room without another word.

As soon as he had gone, a surge of panic washed over me. I'd met my father and hadn't said one thing I'd meant to. When would I have the chance to speak to him again? I walked out into the hallway in time to see him leading Maren by the elbow into another waiting room two doors down the hallway.

I hurried down the hall, but then paused in front of the door. It was open a sliver, but I didn't go inside. What would I say? Should I wait until he came out to try and talk to him?

I opened the door a bit more, but neither of them noticed me. They stood face-to-face, oblivious to interruptions. Alex Kingsley's hands were on his hips. Maren's were folded across her chest. Their voices were low, but as fierce as if they'd been yelling.

Maren said, "I'm taking care of Kari's reputation while she gets help. Do you really want the tabloids parading her problems out for the whole nation to see? Do you want Kari Kingsley jokes told on the late-night programs for the next ten years? What will that do for her career? What will that do to her as a person? You should thank me for this. I did it for you."

He gave her a daggered look. "When I told you to keep an eye on her, this wasn't what I wanted, and you know it. I bailed that girl out of her bad decisions for years, and the reason she hasn't changed yet is that whenever she makes a mess of things, there's always someone else around to clean it up for her. She doesn't need more people to rescue her, she needs to grow up and take responsibility for herself. If that means she has to cancel a concert and refund some money—so be it."

I should have spoken, cleared my throat—done something to let them know I stood in the doorway. But I didn't. I didn't even open the door further. I couldn't intrude on such a heated conversation. Besides, watching Alex Kingsley speak hypnotized me into silence.

Maren stepped toward him, hands upward. "There's no

need to cancel the concert now. Kari's double can do the job. The fans will be much happier that way."

He cocked his head in disbelief. "You're worried about the fans? Can you imagine what the press would say if they caught wind of a fake performing her concert?"

Maren shrugged as though it didn't matter. "If you want, I'll fire the double, but she's been performing as Kari for weeks. She'll keep quiet about this. I'll make sure of it."

I could see him clench his jaw, but he didn't yell at her. His voice came out with taut restraint. "You go let the crowd know that Kari can't do the concert and they're entitled to a refund. If they want to stick around—fine. I'll sing a few songs for them and might be able to talk Grant into doing a few too. Go do it now. We'll discuss your lack of judgment later."

His words snapped me out of my trance. I didn't want them to see me in the doorway and realize I'd listened to the whole thing. I turned and hurried back down the hallway to the green room.

I needed to figure out what to do next. Alex Kingsley would be here for a while. What would be the best way to talk to him, to explain why I'd done all this? A minute later, Maren flung the door open and stormed over to me. Before I knew what was happening, she drew back her hand and slapped me.

I stared at her openmouthed, stung as much by surprise as by the force of her blow. I hadn't thought professional women actually slapped people. The old Alexia might have slapped her back, but I had no desire to do it now. I was better than that.

"That's for being *so . . . incredibly . . . stupid*," Maren hissed at me. "Everything would have worked out fine if you'd done your job and stayed away from Grant Delray. But no, you couldn't be happy with the money—you had to go for other perks. And now you've ruined everything." I hadn't thought her eyes could grow harder, but they did. "You're finished. Your driver will take you to the airport. Get on the next plane to West Virginia and never tell anyone about any of this. If you do—"

"You'll charge me with identity theft," I finished for her.

She smiled with satisfaction, and I wondered how she could do that—go from yelling to a smile like nothing existed in between. "You're getting smarter already." She turned on her heel and went out the door before I could say anything else.

I put my hand to my cheek trying to erase the throb of her slap. How long did I have until security escorted me to the car? I looked around for my street clothes and saw them sitting on the counter. I had started toward them when the door opened. I expected it to be Maren again, giving me more departure instructions. Instead Alex Kingsley stepped into the room. Anger laced his expression, but his voice stayed even. "We're canceling the concert and Kari won't need a double anymore, so you can go on home." He eyed me over, and a muscle twitched near his jaw. "Besides leading on Grant, what else did you do while you were pretending to be my daughter?"

I stared back at him without flinching. "I lip-synched songs, signed autographs, and visited a hospital full of sick kids."

He gave a humorless laugh. "Is that how you justified this to yourself—you visited sick kids, so it was okay to swindle thousands of people? You're lucky I don't turn the two of you in to the police and let everyone know what you've done. I swear I would, except I think Maren really meant to help, and you look too much like my daughter for me to haul you off to jail." His gaze ran over me again. "It's downright eerie. But I will tell you one thing—that money you brought in—it's going to charity. Neither you nor Kari is keeping a dime of it." He threw me one last disdainful gaze. "And I'll give you a piece of advice, young lady. Next time you take a job, make sure you bring your ethics along."

In all my fantasies about meeting my father, not once did I ever think he'd be chewing me out. Everything I'd planned to say to him, my thoughts of being either forgiving or aloof evaporated from my mind. I was angry, and I wanted to hurt him. "Maybe I inherited my sense of ethics from my father."

"Your father? Who's that?"

"You'd do better to ask who my mother is."

He tilted his chin down, humoring me. "Fine. Who's your mother?"

I said the words slowly, waiting to see every inch of his reaction. "Sabrina Garcia."

No recognition passed through his eyes. None. I hated him at that moment.

He shrugged, annoyance creeping into his voice. "Should I know who that is?"

"Yes, you should." I put one hand on my hip. "Ask me who my father is again."

His gaze drifted up to the wall clock. "Listen, I've said what I came to say to you—"

"But I haven't," I cut him off. "You're my father. You. Alex Kingsley."

Instead of registering any shock, he raised his eyebrows and chuckled. "Miss, you've got a bad case of believing your own press. You're not Kari, and I've never seen you before in my life."

I dropped my hand from my hip. "You're right, you've never seen me. That's my whole point. You were never there for me." I took several steps toward him before I pulled the necklace from around my neck. I held it up to him, letting it dangle between my fingers. "You met my mother in Charleston nineteen years ago." His gaze locked onto the pendant, and I could tell he recognized it. His eyes swept back over to mine, and the color drained from his face.

I took one last step toward him, holding the chain out. "This was never meant for me, so you can have it back." I dropped the necklace into his hand without taking my eyes from his. "My mother raised me by herself. She tried to reach you, tried to tell you that you had another daughter. She couldn't even get through. You were a big star, and she was nothing to you. But I did fine without you." I felt the tears rimming my eyes, stinging, and I attempted unsuccessfully to keep them from coming. "I'm a straight-A student," I said to prove my point. "I'm in the National Honor Society at my school. That's how Maren found me. She saw my NHS picture and thought the school was posting pictures of Kari. When she asked if I would double for Kari, I said I'd do it on one condition—that I got to meet you. I wanted to know what you were like. I wanted to meet my father."

He stared at me, stunned, and didn't say a thing. The tears spilled onto my cheeks, but I didn't wipe them away. "And I don't care what you do with the money. I didn't do this for the money. I wanted to help Kari, and okay, maybe I wanted to know what it felt like to be famous too, to be your daughter for real, but I don't need Kari's money, I don't need your money—" My voice faltered, emotion strangling my words until I could barely speak. "And I don't need you, either, so I don't care that you don't love me. I'm fine without you."

He moved then, almost as though the shock had passed and he could react again. He reached out and pulled me into a hug. His arms shook, or perhaps that was just me, still shuddering with emotion. "I don't need you," I choked out. "I don't need you." I said it over and over again, each time becoming less comprehensible until I was sobbing into his shirt.

He held me tight, and when I finished telling him I didn't need him, he spoke softly into my hair. "No one ever told me. I'm so sorry. I would have been there for you if I had known."

I laid my cheek against his shirt, letting the emotion bleed dry. I could feel each breath he took. He was my father, and he had his arms around me. He cared about me. It was a safe feeling. It was all I had ever wanted.

And then I imagined him holding my mother like this. She had thought he cared about her too.

I pushed away from him, my resentment flaring back. "You never called my mother," I said. "She gave you her phone number. She was in love with you, and you never even called her. She had to give up her dreams of going to college. It changed her whole life."

He kept his eyes on me like he was memorizing my features and slowly shook his head. "I put her number in my jeans pocket and then forgot about it and sent it through the wash. All I remembered was that her name was Sabrina and she lived in West Virginia." He lifted a hand and then let it fall. "I didn't think it would matter that much to her."

"That's just great," I said. "I went through my entire childhood without a father because you're lousy at laundry and didn't think any of it mattered."

"I'm sorry," he said again. "I didn't mean for this to happen."

I wiped my face to clear the tears off my cheeks. "It mattered," I said, and suddenly felt drained. I'd wanted to hear exactly what he'd said—that he was sorry and that he would have been there for me. I thought hearing those words would fill the empty places inside me, but I wasn't even sure I believed him.

I said, "Maren told the driver to take me to the airport. I've got to change my clothes now."

"Don't go yet," he said. "I just met you."

I shook my head and picked up my street clothes from the counter. "I still have some stuff at Maren's. If I don't see her before I leave, can you ask her to send the schoolbooks back? I don't care about the rest of it."

"You don't have to leave."

"I've had enough of Hollywood. If you want to talk to me sometime, my mother is listed in the phone book. Sabrina Garcia, Morgantown, West Virginia."

"I want to talk to you now."

I turned and walked away from him, heading to the back of the room where the private bathroom was. As I reached for the doorknob, he said, "You haven't even told me your name."

I turned back to glance at him. "Alexia." I watched the word hit its mark. He understood the significance. Then I went into the bathroom and locked the door.

I glanced in the mirror. I expected to look like a mess, with mascara stains running down my face. It had stayed put pretty well, though. I guess using high-priced water-proof makeup did have its advantages.

I undid my zipper and slid out of my skirt. I thought

he'd left, but then I heard his voice close to the door. "Look, I know you have a right to be angry, but this isn't completely my fault. I didn't know about you. I had no idea."

I pulled off the leotard with more viciousness than I should have. I didn't want to be Kari anymore. If I could have yanked away the blond hair color and the extensions, I would have done that too. "When my mom got hold of your manager, he called her a gold digger and told her to leave you alone. She didn't press it after that because she didn't want me to get hurt if you rejected me like you'd rejected her."

He swore loud enough that I heard it through the door. "I wouldn't have rejected you," he said, "and I didn't mean to reject her, either."

I should have been happy to hear this, but I thought about all the times I'd wanted a dad so badly; all the hurt I'd had to struggle through. My pain had been for nothing. None of it needed to happen.

There was silence while I pulled on my shirt and jeans, and then his voice came again, this time sounding softer. "Do you sing?"

I bent down to put on my shoes. "Not as well as you or Kari."

"Are you going to college?"

"WVU offered me a scholarship."

"What are you majoring in?"

I tied my first shoe slowly. "I don't know. Maybe biology, maybe physics."

"Physics?" He let out a low whistle. "You must get that from your mother."

I didn't answer. To tell the truth, I didn't know if she had liked physics or not.

"How is your mother?" he asked.

I tied my last shoe. "Good. Busy. She's working and finishing her business degree. She's had to support my grandmother and me, but she's always been there for us. She worries about me a lot."

"Good," he said, but I wasn't sure what he approved of.

I smoothed down my hair, trying to shake as much glitter out of it as I could, then I stepped out of the bathroom.

He was waiting by the door, his hands in his pockets. He opened his mouth to speak, but before he could, the dressing room door swung open and Maren stepped in. Her gaze ricocheted between my father and me, then settled on me. "The driver is ready for you."

I folded my arms and didn't move just to show her I wasn't taking orders from her anymore.

"Maren," my father said. "I'm glad you're here. I want to ask you a favor."

"Anything." Her voice grew smooth and soft again. "Really, I'm so sorry about this—I was trying to help Kari—"

"I know," he said. "And that's why I know you'll be able to handle things with Alexia."

"I've already taken care of it." She slid a challenging glance in my direction. "Alexia knows her place."

He stepped over to me, putting his hand on my shoulder.

"No, I don't think she does, but I want to make it clear to her." To Maren he said, "You didn't know this before, but Alexia is my daughter."

The smile froze on Maren's face. She didn't look at me, just blinked at my father. "What?"

"She's Kari's half sister. I just found out myself."

Maren still stared at my father. Her voice came out high-pitched. "What?"

My father smiled, appraising me again. "It's incredible, isn't it? Can you believe how much she looks like Kari?"

Maren stepped toward him but her gaze sliced over to me. "She can't possibly be your daughter. It's a fluke that she looks like Kari—" She let out a sound that was half scoff, half snort. "Whatever she's told you, it isn't true. I found her in *West Virginia*, for heaven's sake."

My father nodded. "West Virginia, I know. That's where I found her mother too." He opened his hand and turned the sapphire pendant over in his palm. His eyes went to mine, and his voice dropped. "You tell your mom I'm sorry. Tell her—well, I'll give her a call myself." He slipped the necklace into his pocket and faced Maren again. "I imagine Kari will have to let most of her staff go until she can get her finances back in order, but I'd like to hire you to do some things. First, I want you to make sure Alexia has a first-class ticket to get back to West Virginia; a private plane would be better. I don't want her bothered while she's traveling. And pack up and send Alexia's belongings back to her house. Can you manage that?"

Maren took a couple of breaths, then gulped. Her voice, usually so silky, cracked. "Of course. I'll take care of it right away."

"Great," he said, "because I've got some people to sing to." He gave my shoulder a pat and then in lower voice said, "I will call you."

He turned to go, but before he could leave, I said, "Can I ask you for one thing?"

"Sure. Anything."

"Can you explain this to Grant?"

He raised an eyebrow. "Wouldn't you rather do that yourself?"

I shook my head. Grant had already made himself clear about what he wanted in a girlfriend, and I didn't fit the bill.

"Okay," he said, but his eyebrow stayed raised like he didn't believe me.

"One more thing." I grabbed my purse from the counter, pulled out a pen, then walked over to my father. I took hold of his hand and turned it over in my own until I could see his forearm. Then I wrote my home phone number in one-inch lettering up the length of his arm. "That's so you don't lose it."

He took my hand and squeezed it. "I won't."

I gave him a smile, then walked to where Maren stood in the doorway. "I'm ready to go now."

CHAPTER 16

As soon as the limo pulled away from the coliseum, Maren turned and stared at me. I had seen and talked to her hundreds of times since I came to California, but this was the first time I'd ever seen her flustered.

"So," she said, "is it actually true you're his daughter?"

I suppose I deserved that comment after spending the last month and a half lying to people about my identity. "It's true," I said.

Her lips pursed together. "Really? And who is your mother? Why didn't this surface before?"

Out the window I could see cars passing by as though the world hadn't just changed. It seemed odd when everything felt different for me. I wasn't even upset about the things Maren had said earlier or was saying now. Suddenly she didn't seem very significant. "My father knows who my mother is. I don't have to explain anything to you."

Maren leaned back against her seat, turning to see me better. "So you're saying it was a coincidence that I picked you—Alex Kingsley's secret daughter—out of the millions of girls in America to be Kari's double?"

"It wasn't coincidence," I said. "You picked me because I looked like her, and I looked like her because she's my half sister. Our mothers resembled each other too. If he wants a

DNA test for proof, that's fine. But I doubt he'll ask for one. He knows who I am."

I think it was at this moment that Maren believed me. She let out a sharp breath and laughed. Not regular laughter—uncomfortable, stumbling laughter.

"Well, isn't that ironic. All this time. You're his daughter." She put her hand over her chest as though checking to make sure her heart was still beating. "You should have confided in me from the beginning. Things would have been different."

"Oh. You mean like you wouldn't have slapped me back in the green room?"

She winced. "I'm sorry about that. It was the stress of the moment. If I had known you were Alex's daughter—"

"Then you wouldn't have threatened to press charges against me if I crossed you?"

She attempted a smile. "I think we got off on the wrong foot."

"The wrong foot? I've lived under your roof long enough to know you don't have any right feet."

She gave a little laugh as though I'd been joking and unclipped her phone from her belt. "I'd better see about getting you a plane to West Virginia."

I didn't mind the break in the conversation. I called my house. Mom was out with Larry, so I told Abuela I was on my way home and would get the flight information to her later.

After several minutes on the phone, Maren wrote down

an airline and flight number on a piece of scratch paper and handed it to me. "You'll be in first class on the next flight out. I'll send your things to you tomorrow."

When the limo finally pulled up to the airport, Maren leaned over and put a hand on my arm. She might have been talking to Kari for all the sweetness in her voice. "Really, Alexia, I would have helped you. I still want to help you. So we should forget the past, especially certain . . . regrettable parts."

I stepped out of the car, pulling my arm away from her as I did. "Thanks for your help. But I'm still going to tell my father everything you've done."

CHAPTER 17

The flight was long, made longer by the fact that people in the airport kept staring and whispering. Several people came up and asked for my autograph. "I'm not Kari Kingsley," I told them. "I'm her sister."

I didn't explain about the glitter in my hair. I figured they could think it was a family trait. We all glittered, just like the Cullens in *Twilight*.

Oddly enough, they still wanted my autograph. "That's so cool," one said. "Do you get to tour with her and meet celebrities and stuff?"

That's when it hit me that going back to being Alexia Garcia might be more complicated than just dyeing my hair brown again. I didn't want to give them a lot of personal information, so I said, "Sometimes."

All during the flight I worried that Abuela might not have been able to get hold of my mother with my flight information and I'd have to take a cab to my house, but when I got to the airport, Mom stood waiting by the baggage carousel. I could see the lines of worry etched on her face as she searched the crowd, and then her eyes flew open wide when she recognized me. She hurried over and hugged me. "Your hair is so long—just look at you! You look—"

"Exactly like Kari, I know."

"I was going to say older." She held me at arm's length, looking me up and down. "And more . . . I don't know, like such a sophisticated lady."

"It's the clothes."

She led me a few paces away so we weren't standing by the crowd. "So tell me everything. Did you ever get to meet him?"

"I met him right before I left. He was really nice."

"Really?" she asked, but she sounded more alarmed than pleased. "Are you going to see him again?"

I shrugged. "He said he'd call me, so I hope so."

"*He said he'd call you?*" The words dropped from her mouth in disbelief, and I knew what she thought. He had said he would call her too.

"Mom, he left your phone number in his jeans pocket and accidentally sent it through the wash. He didn't have any way to reach you. And his manager never told him about your phone call. He didn't know about your pregnancy."

She blinked repeatedly like she didn't know what to make of my words, like she couldn't take them in. The years of not having a father stretched before me again, and this time I wasn't sure whom I felt worse for, my mother or me. Perhaps I shouldn't have said it, but I added, "Why didn't you try to contact him again? You wouldn't have had to tell me about it if he had rejected us. Why didn't you at least try?"

She tore her gaze away from me and swallowed hard. She stared at the baggage carousel for several seconds before she turned to me again. "I always told myself I kept the truth from you because I didn't want you to get hurt, but when I saw you walk up just now, looking like you belonged in Beverly Hills—well, that wasn't the whole reason. I can't compete with him, Lexi. He can buy you anything and take you anywhere. What child would want to live with her poor, struggling mother when she could live with her famous, rich father? You're my whole life. I didn't want him to come and take you away."

Her eyes teared up, and I pulled her into a hug. "I wouldn't have . . . ," I said, but I couldn't finish the sentence. *I wouldn't have left you for money.* Up until I went to California I had been too preoccupied with my lack of money, my secondhand clothes, and my small house. I'd been so eager to make a bundle of cash for being Kari's double. If my father and mother had had joint custody of me all along, would I have been too ashamed to live with my mother?

"The money doesn't matter," I said. "No one has ever loved me as much as you have. Nothing is going to change that."

She held me tighter, put her head against my shoulder, and cried.

• • •

Mom took me to a salon the next day to dye my hair back to brown. I only felt a twinge of guilt that I was covering Peter the Hungarian hairstylist's highlighting masterpiece.

I was ready to be a brunette again. I had the beautician dye the hair extensions along with my hair. I decided I wanted long hair, after all.

I had expected that once my hair turned brown again, I'd look pretty much like I had before I left for California. I'd only been gone two months. But even as I peered in the mirror, I couldn't find the old Alexia. Mom was right. I seemed older. Or maybe it was just that I felt so different.

All day long, I kept finding bits of glitter scattered throughout the house. They turned up on the bathroom counter and kitchen table like little fairy gifts. They didn't bother me so much now. I knew they wouldn't last.

I spent most of Sunday sitting on our worn and fraying couch telling Mom and Abuela everything that happened. It was good to be home. Instead of being ashamed of our cramped kitchen and the family portraits that hung in cheap frames on the wall, I found I didn't want to change any of it. It was comfortable and cozy, unpretentious and warm, like Mom and Abuela.

Abuela for once was more interested in listening than talking. She loved how I told Alex Kingsley that he was my father after he'd lectured me on ethics. They both felt sorry for Kari. Mom felt sorry for Kari because she'd had such a hard life, and Abuela felt sorry for Kari because she'd had such an easy one. Mom said she'd remember Kari in her prayers. Abuela offered to teach her Spanish.

When I laughed at the idea, Abuela pulled herself up straighter and said, "And why shouldn't I teach her Span-

ish? If she's your sister, she's family. She's my half granddaughter."

I wondered what Kari would think about such an addi-
tion to her relatives. And then I wondered if she already
knew the truth. When would he tell her? Would she be
happy or horrified?

I also wondered if my father had told Grant about me
yet. How upset would he be that I'd deceived him about my
identity? Would he try and contact me or would he be
happy to let everything about us disappear?

The phone rang, and Abuela, Mom, and I looked at it,
then looked at each other. "You get it," I said to Mom.

She didn't move. "If that's your father, he's calling to talk
to you, not me. You get it."

"Mom, he said he wanted to talk to you. You should
get it."

"I'm not going to answer it."

Abuela stood up. "*I'll* get it. I have a thing or two to say
to that man."

Which made Mom and I both dive for the phone. I got
to it first, answering with a breathless "Hello?"

It wasn't my father or Grant. A man's voice I didn't recognize asked to speak to my mother. I handed her the
phone. After a few moments, I could pick up from the
conversation that it was my father's lawyer. He wanted
the name of Mom's lawyer—as though we naturally had
one. Something to do with back child support. The whole
topic made Mom uncomfortable, and she paced around the

kitchen while she talked. After she hung up, she said to Abuela, "I don't know how to handle this. I didn't raise my daughter because I thought someday he'd pay me for it."

"Don't look a gift check in the mouth," Abuela said. "You've still got to send Lexi to college." Abuela brushed a piece of lint from her housedress. "And if we have enough left over to take a cruise, *bueno*. Who's to say we don't deserve it?"

I waited for the phone to ring again. And I knew, though she didn't say it, that my mom waited too. Certainly if my father's lawyer called today, my father would call too. He'd call to talk about money stuff with my mom or to make sure I got home okay. Something.

Lori came over that evening. She loved my hair's new length. I told her my sister had insisted I get it done so we'd have our hair the same way. I didn't tell her any names, though. It would change how everyone saw me, and I was still getting used to the idea of them as family. Besides, it was my mother's secret too, and maybe she didn't want the whole town to find out.

"So do you feel better knowing your father?" Lori asked. "Do you feel more complete?"

"I do feel better," I said, "but probably because it made me realize I was complete to begin with. Knowing who he is doesn't change who I am at all."

Lori passed over this comment like it was self-evident, and maybe it had been to her all along. "Did you meet any cute guys?"

"One."

"And?" she prompted.

"And now I'm probably ruined for dating for the rest of my life. Nobody is going to be able to measure up."

She leaned toward me. "Sounds interesting—what was he like?"

"Handsome, nice, talented. He wrote a song for me, and when he sang it . . ." I sighed. I didn't have words to describe the experience. "He had the most beautiful voice."

"So are you keeping in contact with him?"

I shook my head. "It wouldn't work out. We're from different worlds."

She must have seen how much it hurt to say this. She immediately switched into loyal-friend mode. "Don't worry. I promise you're not ruined for dating." She leaned over and playfully flicked a piece of my hair. "You look great— your hair, makeup, and . . . I don't know, you just have this confident air about you now. It's so . . . I can't put my finger on it."

I could. It was so Kari Kingsley, but I didn't say it.

"Hey, I bet the day after finals Theresa will dump Trevor flat-out," Lori said. "I think she's only dating him because he's smart—you know, geek-farming. He'll be ripe for some consolation."

I smiled at her, but really, the thought of Trevor did nothing for me.

Eventually it grew late and Lori left and I got ready for bed. I stayed up later than I should have. I was still on

California time. It didn't have anything to do with phone calls that never came.

. . .

Monday morning was abruptly depressing. First of all, I was tired. Second, it was gray and rainy, and I was still used to blue California skies. Third, instead of a driver, I had to get out my one-spoke-is-broken-but-it-still-works-anyway umbrella and dodge puddles and worms on the sidewalk going to school. Then I had to explain to the office that I'd returned for the rest of the school year.

Hector waved when he saw me, but didn't do anything odd or stalkerish, so I assumed he was back to normal.

Besides a few of my friends, no one in the hallways even commented on the fact that I'd been absent for so long. It should have felt nice to be invisible for a change, but it didn't. It was almost heartening when Theresa looked me over while I walked to third-period English and said, "You're back. I guess we'll need to watch for flying books in the library again."

Zoey, one of the Cliquistas, said, "Theresa, you'd better keep an eye on Trevor. Alexia has got some temptress hair going. Maybe she'll try to steal him."

Theresa laughed and said, "What *did* you do to your hair? I mean, *really*."

I ignored her, though, glad for once I could chalk it up to sour grapes. Between Peter and the salon, my hair still looked great. I also ignored Trevor when he tried to make small talk in physics class. He practically draped himself over my desk, but I figured if he could dump me without explanation before the Sadie Hawkins dance, then I wasn't required to respond to his flirting. And besides, what sort of guy flirted with me when he was going out with Theresa? They deserved each other.

At lunchtime Trevor sat at Theresa's table and they both looked at me, lowered their voices, and then laughed.

This was the sort of thing I was going to have to endure until graduation. Even though I tried to fight it, my mind kept replaying memories of Grant. The way his eyes crinkled when he laughed. The lilt in his smile when he saw me.

There's something really depressing in knowing that the happiest moments of your life have all come when you were pretending to be someone else.

I dreaded last period, when I'd have to see Trevor in world history, but at the end of fifth period, the principal came on the loudspeakers and announced a school-wide assembly. We were to go immediately to the gym. "And I caution you not to skip out," she said. "Trust me, you don't want to miss this."

Which went to show you how out of touch school faculty was, because I had never been to an assembly that wasn't worth missing. Still, I found Lori and filed into the gymnasium with the rest of the school.

Bleachers lined the wall, but the middle of the floor had

been partitioned off by gym mats turned on their sides to create a screen. These were being held up by teachers so no one could get a look inside. Our only clue to their content was several electric cords that snaked across the floor. The kids sitting behind me spent their time guessing what the assembly would be about. "Definitely a drug assembly," one said. "We're going to hear how we'll die penniless, emaciated, and covered with sores in some crack house if we ever try them."

"Car safety," someone else said. "I bet some idiot crashed during lunchtime and now we get a lecture on wearing safety belts."

I flipped open my calculus notebook and concentrated on my homework. I'd done two problems when the screaming began.

At first I thought something was wrong. Like maybe the bleachers were collapsing or the gym had caught on fire. Then I saw what everyone was gaping at. The teachers had pulled away the mats, revealing a drummer, two guys on electric guitar, a guy on keyboard, and in front of them, rock sensation Grant Delray.

CHAPTER 18

I didn't blame the girls for screaming. He looked that good. He wore white pants and a tight white shirt that emphasized his broad, muscular shoulders. His hair had been gelled back, which accentuated his striking features and square jaw.

I watched him, unable to breathe.

Grant looked up at the bleachers, but if he was searching for me, I couldn't tell. He held up one hand and said, "Hey, everybody, how's it going?"

He might have said more, but since nearly every girl in the gym, including Lori, screamed again, I didn't hear what. Even his microphone headset couldn't overcome that kind of volume.

After the sound died down, he said, "I came to Morgantown to pay someone a visit, and I thought I could stop by and give you a short concert—"

More screaming. Even louder this time, if that was possible.

He smiled and called out, "Let's get it started!"

And just like that, he and the band moved on cue. He wasn't a person now, he was an entertainer, fluid with the beat. When he sang, the music vibrated through me and I couldn't think of anything else. I watched him song after song, mesmerized.

Why had he come here? It seemed like a long way to come to pay a visit. Did it mean he'd forgiven me for lying to him, or was it something else?

As I stared at him, I tried to catch his eye, any little shift of his gaze that would show he saw me. Sometimes when he did more singing than dancing, his eyes seemed to rest on my section of the bleachers, but then the next moment he'd look somewhere else, so I couldn't be sure. Maybe he had trouble picking me out of the crowd with my brown hair.

After about forty-five minutes of performing, he said, "We're going to slow things down now. This is a song I wrote for someone who means a lot, and it would mean even more if she sang it with me." Then he looked directly into my eyes; he'd known where I was all along.

"Alexia," he said, "do you want to come down here?"

En masse, every pair of eyes turned and looked at me. Grant smiled, and I felt myself blush bright pink. Lori nudged my arm. "Oh, my gosh!" she whispered. "Go!"

I stood up, still blushing, and made my way down the bleachers. My heart pounded so hard I could hear it in my ears. I told myself I shouldn't be so rattled. I'd been up in front of bigger crowds than this during the last month. But this was different. I wasn't standing up in front of an audience as Kari Kingsley. I couldn't hide behind her image here—I was facing them as me.

As I made my way across the floor, Grant said to the

crowd, "I sent Alexia the music to this song a week and a half ago. We'll see how well she's practiced it."

I went and stood beside him, feeling his blue-eyed gaze resting on me. I couldn't read his expression. Grant smiled, but there was a stiffness to it, making him look more angry than happy. He handed me a copy of the sheet music. He shouldn't have bothered. I'd memorized the words on the first night he'd sent them.

I didn't glance at the crowd. I couldn't. Instead I gave him a nervous smile and whispered, "I can't believe you're doing this to me."

He reached up to his headset and switched off his mike so the audience wouldn't hear him. "That makes us even, since I can't believe what you did to me either."

The intro started. I glanced down at the paper in my hands to give my eyes someplace to look besides at him. "You know, you've never heard me sing. You're going to be sorry if I'm horrible at this."

"Well, one of us will be sorry." He clipped a microphone onto the collar of my shirt and sent over a challenging look.

Which made me wonder if he could have come all this way just to humiliate me in front of my classmates.

I raised my chin in defiance, and the nervousness drained away. I wanted to prove that I could sing. It would be my voice the audience heard this time, not a lip-synched version of Kari. I held the sheet music down, but still kept my gaze on him.

He turned his mike back on and sang the first line in his beautiful, full voice. When it was my turn, my words came out strong and clear. Melodic.

His eyebrows rose in surprise and then he smiled. A real smile this time.

I admit I had an advantage. I'd practiced to the taped version of him singing this song dozens of times. I knew how to blend my voice with his. He'd never practiced with me. Still he did an amazing job—another proof of his talent.

When we'd finished, he took my hand in his, then pulled me into an embrace. And there in front of the entire school, he bent down and kissed me. Some of the guys in the bleachers howled at that, but I didn't care.

Grant turned back to the bleachers. "Thanks for letting us come," he said. "I've had a really good time."

More catcalls from the bleachers.

This time I glanced at the audience. I couldn't tell who'd been yowling, but my gaze stopped on the front row where Trevor, Theresa, and the Cliquistas stared at me openmouthed.

I smiled at them, then looked away.

Grant waved at the audience, still not letting go of my hand. "You guys have been great!" While the band played a refrain, he turned and pulled me across the gym. One of the teachers had propped open the back door for us.

I barely heard the principal's announcement that everyone should proceed in an orderly manner to their lockers to conclude the school day. The door shut behind us. We were outside and heading toward a dark blue sports car.

"Sorry about the quick exit," Grant said. "I didn't want them to mob us."

Us. Like my schoolmates would ever want to mob me. We climbed into the sports car, and Grant started it up. I looked back at the building. "What about your band?"

"My security guys and the teachers are going to help with crowd control until the guys have the equipment packed up in the van. Fortunately for them, they get fewer teenage girls trying to rip the clothes off their backs." Grant guided the car through the parking lot, and I wondered where we were going. I didn't ask. Really, I didn't care.

When we'd pulled out onto the main street, he turned a penetrating gaze on me. "Why didn't you tell me the truth?"

"Technically, I did."

He let out a grunt of disbelief. "Yeah, right after you asked how my plans for world domination were going. That does not equal a confession."

"I knew if I told you you'd be angry."

His eyes flashed in my direction before he turned his attention back to the road. "You're right. I'm angry. Every time we were together, you lied to me. I keep thinking about how much I miss you, and then I wonder how I can possibly miss you when I never knew who you were to begin with. Which part of you was actually *you* and which part was you pretending to be Kari?"

He glanced over expectantly. He wanted an answer.

"It was all me, except I'm not rich, famous, or especially talented. I also don't gamble, shop obsessively, date Michael Jung, or give concerts."

"You performed at lots of concerts," he said.

"Okay, I'm a pretty good lip-syncher. Oh, and also I'm not a vegetarian."

"Yeah, I had that part figured out." He slowed the car to go around a corner. "I can't believe you went down to the hospital and lied to sick kids about who you were."

"I was trying to make them happy," I said. "Like the way Santa visits people at Christmas. But in a less jolly, more superstar sort of way."

"And why did you date me? Was that to get information on Lorna's book or to create publicity for Kari's CD, or were you just trying to make me happy too—was I part of your goodwill-toward-the-public-on-Kari's-behalf campaign?"

I lowered my voice. "I wasn't supposed to see you. Kari and Maren both told me not to, but I couldn't help myself."

He gripped the steering wheel harder. "And were you ever going to tell me who you really were? Or did that only happen because you got caught?"

Without trying, I could conjure up every memory of our breakup, his words, his expressions. It still hurt. "How could I tell you the truth, when you only liked me because you thought I was Kari Kingsley?"

His gaze momentarily swung around to mine. "Are you kidding? I read the book on Kari, literally. You think I liked her? I was going out of my mind trying to reconcile how the girl in front of me could have done the things Lorna said Kari had done."

He turned onto my street, slowing down as we came to my house. I wondered how he'd known where I lived.

"My band members thought I'd gone insane," he said. "First because I kept telling them I was dating Kari Kingsley—and she was this smart, wonderful girl, only she didn't want to let anybody know we were a couple, so they couldn't meet her—and then that looked like a huge lie, so I had to tell them that, no, actually I'd been dating Kari Kingsley's nearly identical half sister from West Virginia that nobody knew about."

"It was nice of them to come all this way to do a concert for my school."

"Nice had nothing to do with it. They were taking bets on my sanity." He nodded with satisfaction. "They each owe me a hundred bucks."

"Is that why you came? To win a bet?"

Grant pulled into my driveway and turned off the car. He made no move to get out, though.

He had only glanced at my house; still, I couldn't help but see it through his eyes. A small, rundown gray home with worn paneling and a roof that needed repair. I looked at the dashboard so I wouldn't have to see it anymore.

He said, "I came because I wanted to hear about this from you, not secondhand from your father. You owe me that much at least."

"You're right," I said. "I owe you an apology. I'm sorry for every time I lied to you. I hated doing it, but you never would have looked at me, let alone dated me, if you hadn't thought I was a celebrity. You said as much yourself the last time we were together. You said you were glad Kari outclassed you. You said Kari was better than the nameless masses. Well, I'm a certified member of the nameless masses. That's who I am."

He lifted one hand in protest. "I thought you were worried about the backlash from Lorna's book, and I was trying to comfort you. I didn't mean that I wouldn't like you unless you were famous."

My gaze flicked to our house, then back to him. "Celebrities date celebrities. That's just the way it is."

Grant's gaze moved to my house and stayed there. "You mean celebrities use the people who have crushes on them and then never call?"

Which meant he knew the story of my mother and father. "Yes," I said. "Something like that." I reached for the door handle, but he took hold of my arm and pulled me back toward him.

"I know your name, I already have your home number programmed into my cell phone. And I'm calling you right now." Then he leaned over and kissed me.

For days I had been pushing thoughts of him away, willing myself not to feel these emotions. My efforts fell apart right there in the car. I wound my arms around him and kissed him back until I couldn't breathe anymore. I think the only reason I stopped was the sudden fear that my grandmother might be looking out the window. I didn't want her coming outside to smack Grant's car with a Bible.

Grant let go of me and opened his door. "Come on, there's something you need to see."

I got out of the car and followed him across my yard, even though I had no idea what he was talking about.

He stopped on my front porch and waited for me to open the door. As soon as I did, I heard laughter from inside. My mother's laughter. I walked in, and Grant followed. My mother and father were sitting close together on the living room couch, a photo album spread out on their laps.

Abuela was nowhere around, although I could see down the hallway that her bedroom door was shut. Music drifted out of her room. I wondered how my mother had convinced her that she needed privacy.

Mom looked up at me with a lingering smile on her lips. "Oh, good, Lexi is home. I'm showing Alex some of your pictures."

"I love this one of you with the boots." He pointed to a photo where I was about two years old and wore nothing but cowboy boots and a diaper. "Get the fashion basics down, and you can't go wrong."

Mom said, "She wouldn't wear any other shoes until she went to kindergarten."

He let out a deep chuckle. "That's my girl."

I finally got over the shock of seeing him in my living room and stated the obvious. "You're here."

He stood up then and gave me a brief hug. "Your mother and I had a lot to discuss, and I figured it was better to do it in person." His gaze traveled to Grant. "Alexia's been a straight-A student since sixth grade. I just saw her report cards."

Grant nudged my arm. "I'm impressed."

"And Lexi went to regionals for her science fair project last year," Mom added. "I have pictures of that too."

I sent her a forced smile. "You don't have to show him that."

"I want to see it," my father said, and sat down on the couch again. Mom went to the bookshelf and pulled a different photo album out. She flipped through it, then put it on his lap. "There she is with her ribbon."

Grant nodded. "I definitely want your help when I take over the world."

My father looked up at me and patted his shirt pocket. "I have something for you. It's sort of my way of telling you I want to make amends."

It was silly, but at that moment I fully expected him to produce a horse. Instead he handed me a thin rectangular box and a piece of paper. I opened the box and found a ruby pendant shaped into a heart and surrounded with little diamonds. I turned it to catch the light, and sparkles danced across its surface. It made my breath catch.

"I thought you should have a necklace I picked out just for you," he said. "Do you like it?"

I glanced at my mom to make sure she approved, which is when I noticed she was wearing a new necklace too. Hers had a row of rubies that got progressively bigger until the center stone.

And she had been worried about him spoiling *me*.

"It's beautiful." I took the necklace out of the box, and Grant helped me put it on. Then I looked at the piece of paper.

"It's tickets for you and your family to come out and visit California," my father said.

Mom said, "He has a ranch there. You'd like that." Her voice was so eager, I knew she wanted to go. "He has horses," she emphasized.

"Horses, nothing," my father said. "It's close to Grant." He winked at me, then turned to my mother. "Horses can only sway girls until they're about fifteen. After that, you need guys. That's why I brought him along."

Grant put his hand on my back and smiled. "Say you'll come."

"We'll come," I said.

My father turned to my mother. "See?" And then they both laughed.

I turned to Grant to ask how long he was staying in Morgantown, and that's when I saw Kari and Abuela coming out of her room.

"Kari!" I sputtered.

She walked down the hallway, as casually elegant in my house as she had been in hers. "Your grandma was playing some old Mexican songs for me. They're totally . . ." She looked to my grandmother to supply the word.

"*Qué padre,*" Abuela said, enunciating slowly.

"*Qué padre,*" Kari repeated. "That means awesome." She plopped down on one of the kitchen chairs and tapped her fingers against the table. "I think I want to do a few songs on my next album with that beat."

"I thought you were in Utah," I said.

She picked up a piece of Abuela's homemade fry bread from the table. "When Dad told me he was coming to see you, I checked myself out. Don't worry," she said. "I'm going to finish the program. I just thought it was important to come." She spread some honey butter onto her bread and sent me a severe look. "You really should have told me who you were, Alexia. I can't believe we were together all that time and you never said anything."

"I didn't know how you'd take it." I watched her nibble on the fry bread. "How are you taking it?"

"Well, I wouldn't like finding out that just *anybody* was my sister, but you're cool." She cast a glance at Grant. "Even if your taste in men is lacking."

Grant pulled me closer to him. "She has great taste in men."

Kari smiled mischievously. "Just think of how much fun we can have driving the paparazzi crazy. We'll show up at different events at the same time, and when they report two Kari Kingsley sightings, they'll lose all credibility. Total payback time."

But the thought of the press following me around ignited flames of panic inside my stomach. "Do the paparazzi have to find out about me?"

My father shrugged. "Not if you don't want to tell anyone that you're my daughter. We can try to keep it a secret."

I glanced at my mother, but she shrugged too, turning the decision back over to me.

I felt strangely powerful having the final say. Did I want to live a quiet life as Sabrina Garcia's daughter, or did I want to be known as Alex Kingsley's hidden past? I didn't like the thought of tabloids in every grocery store across America proclaiming to the world what my parents had done, but at the same time, I was so happy that I finally had a father and a sister, that they were here in my living room to see me, that it seemed wrong to keep it a secret. "We can tell people," I said.

He smiled and then went back to looking at the photo album with my mother.

I watched her for a moment, thinking how young she suddenly looked. Poor Larry. His days were numbered.

Grant leaned closer, whispering into my ear, "I think your dad has got her number this time."

I leaned back into him. "I think you're right."

For extra scenes
and other cool content visit
www.janetterallison.com